JUAN CARLOS MÁRQUEZ was born in Bilbao in 1967. He graduated in information science and then studied journalism, but has been a full-time writer and creative writing teacher for several years. He has published three books of short stories, *Norteamérica profunda* (2008), *Oficios* (Castalia, 2008) and *Llenad la Tierra* (2010). He has been nominated twice for the Setenil Prize for Short Fiction, as well as for the prestigious International Ribera del Duero Short Fiction Prize. He has won the José Nogales Prize (2010), the Rafael González Castell Prize (2005) and the Juan Rulfo Prize for the best debut writer (2003). He has appeared in various anthologies in Spain. *Tangram* is his first novel. His second novel, *Los últimos*, was published in 2015.

TANGRAM

Juan Carlos Márquez

Tangram

TRANSLATED BY JAMES WOMACK

Original title: *Tangram*
First published in Spain by Editorial Salto de Página, 2011.
This translation © James Womack 2016

Cover design © Zuri Negrín 2016
This edition © Nevsky Prospects S.L. 2016

http://edicionesnevsky.com

IBIC: FF
ISBN: 978-84-945913-3-4
Legal Registry No.: M-36000-2016
Type: Hoefler Text

Nevsky Books
An imprint of Nevsky Prospects S.L.

2016

Contents

TANGRAM

Each man has a thousand plans for himself.
Fate has only one plan for each man.
Mencius.

I. [Square]

The Basement

I meet Fraile (and we're talking about nearly twenty years ago now) in the Psychology Faculty at Deusto. Fraile is the director of the university theatre group, at whose door I knock at the end of an innocent summer I had spent on some beach in Menorca. Some time back (this is something I need to tell you now), there arose in me, along with my first adolescent erections, a certain inquisitiveness. Under the guidance of Uri Geller and Professor Jiménez del Oso, I become passionately interested in mentalism. I spend my down time with my hands pressed to my temples and my gaze fixed on the flat across from me, trying to cause Doña Reme to become completely naked. I expend so much effort on this that, one evening in May, when I have almost given up hope, I finally see her breasts through the polished glass. This vision, apart from confirming my dedication to the sin of onanism, contributes enormously to a state of, shall we say, self-confidence. For months, which to my parents must seem like years, I am convinced that everything which happens is a result of my will. One morning in August I insist that there will be a snowstorm, and tell my mother. Her reply is a violent slap. Mum! I yelp. So? You could have stopped it with your mental powers, she says. And that is the end of my time as a mentalist. Well, I begin my career as a budding actor under the tutelage of Norberto Fraile with exactly the same degree of enthusiasm.

The fact of belonging to a university theatre group brings with it certain perks. I am referring to groupies, the stalwart supporters who are always on call, most of them uniformed high school students from the institutes where our group tours: the chickenhawk circuit, where we offer a postmodern repertory, the more confusing the better.

If I mention groupies, I don't want you to start thinking about orgiastic sex, drugs and rock'n'roll. None of that, but if things work out right, in the best case scenario, at the end of the night, in a dark alley, the possibility of one's tongue finding shelter in a welcoming mouth is not out of the question.

Via one of these groupies, Norberto gets Dori Galdaretxe's phone number. Dori was a kind of diva in Basque theatre during the seventies, and still has some influential friends, facts which she straightaway broadcasts from the other end of the line. She says that she wants to see us act to get a better idea, and insists that the show must take place in her house, because what with 'her little problem', it's very difficult for her to get around.

The preparation is tiring. Our repertory contains nothing for two actors—we decided in advance not to tell the rest of the company—so we have to display our writing talent and come up with something ourselves, an *entr'acte*. We are sunk deep in the theatre of the absurd, and our play deals with a story that takes place in Louisiana in the middle of the nineteenth century: Tom Strawberry, a slaveholding landowner, lives in a house with Eleanor, his beautiful, delicate and anodyne wife. On Thanksgiving Eve a meteorite falls close to their house. In the morning, Tom looks in the mirror and discovers, to his horror, that his skin has grown noticeably darker; also, Eleanor cannot believe her eyes: an immense penis has sprouted between her legs, so large that she finds it difficult to stand upright. From this moment on, both of them conceive an uncontrollable passion for the poetry of Saint John of the Cross. Norberto will start out by playing Eleanor, and I will be Tom; in the middle of the play we will switch roles.

Dori Galdaretxe lives in a *palazzo* in Neguri, one of those neo-colonial buildings with a garden that adds distinction to a beautiful avenue that runs along the coast. Norberto parks his father's Mercedes at a nearby roundabout and we walk the rest of the way. March is doing its thing. It's a windy afternoon, the sea choppy and a fine rain filling the air. Norberto is wearing a black suit, boots and the inevitable spotted scarf round his neck. This accessory, which he bought in Paris, gives him an air of being an intellectual and an exile. Yours truly, always the sidekick, is carrying the bag of props, which include a tin of shoe polish, a blonde wig, a nightgown and a long pink sausage-shaped balloon. We walk hurriedly, sharing an umbrella that is at the mercy of the wind: an image in which a pretentious writer might find an eloquent metaphor for youth and friendship.

The *palazzo* has a black iron fence protecting it, and in search of a bell we walk almost all the way around its perimeter. When we finally discover it, sticking out of a little cushion of moss, Norberto thrusts the umbrella into my hands and tackles the button. A woman's indomitable voice invites us to come through. It is a gentle yet savage voice, like an affectionate dog might have, and it stays in my ears for a while even after it has stopped. This occurs barely a second before a metal door opens in our faces and we are confronted by a legion of weeds and beech trees whose bunchy roots spread out and cross in all directions. I say that Poe would have loved to take tea in this garden. With Luana Varsavsky, Norberto adds. (Luana Varsavsky is the ugliest girl in the whole university, a six-foot tall freak with lizard eyes and hair on the palms of her hands. Scary.) Then we walk across the garden without looking where we are going, while the rain and the wind get stronger and turn everything into a quagmire. The door to the house is open, and there is a row of little reddish bulbs in the roof of the porch. At the end of a corridor we see some frosted glass doors, the kind that open *ipso facto* in anyone's presence. It does not take us long to go through them and find Dori Galdaretxe and 'her little problem': she is morbidly obese, confined to a double bed, a huge cart for fat people, cutting-edge technology with a motor and four wheels.

Imagine for a moment that Rubens had wanted to paint the Three Graces as a single person: the resulting sketch would have been something like Dori Galdaretxe. Perhaps that's the most humane thing to be said about her. Her weight has wiped any expression from her face, and her eyes, scarcely two sluggish cracks, seem to be looking at you from the base of a cliff made out of fat. She looks vaguely like a hibernating prehistoric animal. However, no one in his right mind would say that she was old. She had stopped dead at some indefinite age between forty and fifty, as if the subsequent years had simply piled one on top of another on her elastic belly.

Dori greets us. She squeezes our hands with her own soft fingers and suggests that I put the costumes and the umbrella that I have just set down on the floor onto a kind of rack under her bed-cum-car. Then we get on a goods lift and follow her down to the cellar. She had constructed a little stage down there for one of her nieces who liked puppets, but the niece had grown up and had turned into the groupie who recommended us to her. The girl, apparently, reminds Dori of herself when she was younger. She also thinks that Norberto is similar to some guy called Gaetano. Gaetano Iabichino. A real asshole, she says. Norberto is almost blushing at his reflection in the goods lift mirror. Did you know we were married? Dori continues. Dori and Gaetano. Gaetano and Dori. *Cat on a Hot Tin Roof. The Long, Hot Summer.* For months we were the toast of half of Europe. Life was marvellous to begin with, and I had a waist. *Porca miseria.* It's difficult to follow Galdaretxe. She leaps from one topic to the next with absolute naturalness, as if she were a pollinating bee leaping from flower to flower.

From the immediate present to the most distant past, and vice-versa. Time falls, half-chewed, from her mouth, but bits are still stuck between her teeth.

The goods lift stops suddenly; the doors open and Norberto and I step out. It is very dark. We can't find anything that even resembles a light switch even by touching the walls all over. Dori Galdaretxe, from inside the goods lift, gives us vague instructions about where it might be. I'm sorry, lads, she says after several attempts, but I haven't been down here for a while. My memory is not what it once was. When I was working I could learn the whole of Joan of Arc at one go, but now... In the few seconds that she does manage to keep her mouth shut, we hear a buzzing noise. It is very irritating. It could be the hum of some domestic appliance, or a heating pipe with some sort of problem, or else an insect colony. Suddenly, Norberto bumps into a huge box, a baby wardrobe or something similar, next to a wall at the far end of the cellar. The blow provokes a common swearword and a metallic clang. It's cold, he shouts. I imagine his elbow or knee in pain as he creeps slowly back towards the object. It's a freezer, he adds. And by then the goods lift had started up again with a groan behind me, headed back up to the ground floor. She'll have gone up for a lantern or something, he says as he heaves up the two heavy lids of the freezer. It is filled to the brim with meat and drink, with a bright white light spilling out of its insides that illuminates the rest of the basement. It's one of those metal chests with two compartments that you're always finding in petrol stations or ice-cream parlours. One side is piled up with cans of drink and little bottles of beer, the other is filled with steaks and chops and ribs and guts wrapped in plastic. For someone like Norberto, who's nearly completely vegetarian, it doesn't seem a very edifying spectacle. He looks like he's about to get an attack of the heaves. The rest of the cellar is no picture, either; apart from the initial joy that we feel on finding matches and candles and a couple of Zamora blankets, what we do is pick bitterly over the abandoned books and useless junk accumulated here—a paperweight, some wire, etcetera—trying at all costs not to say the word 'kidnapped' out loud. There has been not a sign of Dori Galdaretxe for more than half an hour. Also, the button to call the lift has stopped working, and our cries for help bounce uselessly off the walls. All evidence would seem to suggest that on this non-existent stage, the only puppets are ourselves.

At Norberto's suggestion, we spread a blanket on the floor and sit down to talk about our situation by the light of a candle like two Apache chiefs. I personally would like to set fire to the whole place or else run my head against the walls and the ceiling to see just how solid they really are. Alright, Norberto murmurs, we are psychology students and as such we cannot let ourselves get overwhelmed by the situation, that's point one. Point two: we are trapped here and for the time being there's no way around that: the goods lift is solid, there's not a single fucking window, and we don't fit through the ventilation ducts. Point three: if we start shouting it would be easier for them to hear us in the centre of the Earth than in the next-door house. We're agreed up to this point, right? I say yes. Norberto takes the spotted handkerchief out from where it is tucked into his neck, and wipes away a drop of sweat that is running down his left cheek. Point number four, he continues, and this is the most worrying thing: we don't know how long this is going to last. Did you tell anyone that we were coming here? No, I reply in annoyance, we thought that it was a secret. What about you? Norberto shakes his head no. Suddenly I feel the need to get up. Where the fuck are you going? he asks, we haven't finished here. I'm going to get a couple of beers. A well-kept secret, I add. We should celebrate.

That night each of us sleeps wrapped up in his own blanket, head resting on a pile of books. Believe me when I say that literature is growing ever harder, and that sleeping on piles of fiction does not always provoke pleasant dreams. Dori Galdaretxe comes to see me in the night, driving her carriage. Norberto is with me, but his face is a little different: a madman's face, something like that. His eyes are bulging and drool is running freely down his chin. Dori turns to me in an almost friendly way. She wants us to take her wheelchair round the world, so she's added a couple of wings, a mast and a selection of sails. You and me, she says. Alone, without this idiot. And when she finishes saying this she is another Dori: a beautiful girl. Then I say yes, and she turns back into the same morbidly obese woman as before. I try to withdraw my acceptance, but she grabs me like I was weightless and puts me between her legs. And she keeps me like this, a prisoner, until we get to the border between India and Nepal, with the snow and the peaks in the background. Some Indian soldiers want to inspect the chair, and as a preventative measure, Dori hides me inside her vagina. It is a soft and sticky labyrinth, hot as hell. That's as much as I remember. When I wake up, the sweat is streaming off me.

There's not a lot to do in the basement, so most of the time we sleep or remain sunk in a state of lethargy. As the days go by, our eyes become accustomed to the dark; the ever-present stink, a mixture of one's own smell and someone else's, becomes bearable. The matches and the candles are precious goods, and we value them as such. The same match is used to light a candle and to cover up the smell of a turd, and the same candle is used to generate multipurpose wax and light hundreds of fires. The books feed the fire, and the fire cooks the meat. I beat out the steaks with the paperweight, and when they are thin enough to be slipped under a door, Norberto cuts them in strips with the knife from his nail-clippers—luckily he had them attached to his key ring—and then impales the pieces on a wire. A steak and a drink are all that we allow ourselves to eat each day, and there are, more or less, drinks and steaks enough in the freezer for a month.

The first two days, Norberto doesn't eat a mouthful, but on the third day he eats at a sitting three days' worth of food. It's like eating your own tonsils, he says as he forces the first mouthful down. However, the survival instinct overcomes the initial repulsion and as time goes by Norberto even develops his own tastes: 'I want mine crunchy on the outside and raw on the inside,' he says barely a week later, his handkerchief tucked into his collar like a napkin.

It's not all about survival. There's also time for other business. Norberto rigs up some kind of exercise bench and we both spend a while every afternoon spinning around. We learn how to twist and move around in the darkness with the agility and silence of a Chinese puppet theatre. At dawn, a cloudy shaft of light filters through the ventilation grille, and a kind of high-angle light falls on the floor. And we kneel by the light in order to improvise. Norberto calls this play-acting *The Kidnap Show*, a live tragicomedy without an audience or any fixed time for the curtain to come up.

On the other hand, nights are an eternity for Norberto. For all that we try to keep it together, it's impossible not to despair every now and then. The hum of the freezer doesn't stop for a single moment and from time to time one can hear the rain on the windows of the floor above, or else feels at a distance the wind blowing the dead leaves from one end of the garden to the other. There are no other sounds, and it is this absence of noise that makes me feel scared. Oddly enough, my dreams become fairly agreeable, sometimes even pleasant. I dream that I am flying, that I am flapping my arms and flying over unknown cities and cotton fields, and that people wave to me as I pass. Or else I dream that I am walking over a lime-green sea, my pockets filled with seaweed. In one dream I go into a wood and lose myself. I am a little confused and suddenly the trees turn into beautiful women who start to argue about which one of them will take me to bed that night. All my dreams are of open spaces. The nightmares begin when I wake up. I want so much to be free that I hysterically throw myself at the cellar walls and scratch at them in the middle of the night. Until Norberto comes to calm me down, I carry on scratching at the damn walls with my fingertips stained in blood and plaster. Scratching at the walls and crying.

On the eleventh day of our captivity, Norberto stretches at random into the meat freezer and pulls out a hand, cut off at the wrist. It is a man's hand, large and hairy, wrapped in plastic like the rest of the provisions. In a reflex action, Norberto throws it to the other end of the cellar and, after retching a couple of times, heads into a corner to throw up. I'm standing up, gathering some pieces of paper to light the fire, and I drop them and they spread out all over the floor. If I'm right, and if this isn't some kind of sick joke, then we have already eaten more than half of an adult human male. This is what I inform Norberto, with mathematical exactitude, provoking another bout of retching.

The hand keeps us at arm's length for the rest of the day. It divides the basement into two spaces. It's just a piece of dead meat, but to us it's as lively as a recently hooked fish. We don't want to see it, but it's impossible not to look at it. The hand is open, pinkish, its nails and joints intact. It keeps on opening and closing doors in our minds. Even after it has been devoured by the fire and reduced to soot and ashes, it is still present. Even today I don't hold out my hand to strangers, and when there is no option, then I feel myself blushing and my knees begin to tremble, and whenever I see a one-armed man I cross the road.

The next few days we spend sick with some kind of stomach flu, an occurrence—Norberto calls it a blessing—which leaves up in the air the problem of whether or not to eat human flesh. Our faces turn a greenish yellow colour, we throw up five or six times a day—a creamy pap with specks of blood in it— and we shiver in feverish delirium. The fever we suffer from is like one of those hammers that people use in funfairs to test their strength. Suddenly, the hammer hits its bed, and your temperature shoots up to the roof. We have each lost several kilos, eight or ten each, and the flu manages to shake off the few remaining shreds of flesh that hang on our bones. We are squalid, starving—thin would be a kind word for us—and when we go to sleep we need to spend a long time finding a place to lie so as not to damage our hips or pelvis or spine. We hydrate ourselves with unwelcome sips of Coke or Lemon Fanta and when the fever is at its height, Norberto's handkerchief, filled with chips of ice and passed over our foreheads, provides moments that bring us close to ecstasy.

While the sickness lasts, my main preoccupation, in a sudden onset of egotism, is to die first and rest in peace. I imagine myself in this dump with Norberto's corpse rotting under a blanket and tears run down my cheek. I also hear a voice in my head, a deep and dark voice, that tells me what to do in case Norberto does die first, to cut my friend up with the little knife from the nail scissors and put the body in the freezer. Anyway, tears run down my cheeks. In the worst moments, I give myself up to fantasy. The light that filters through the ventilation grille every morning takes on a spiritual tone. Suddenly, I am caught up in this little stream of light and carried away to another dimension, like all those aliens who, after carrying out a secret and dangerous mission on Earth flash back to their home planet almost instantaneously. The cockroaches, which surround our sickbeds when the illness is at its height, belong to a superior civilisation, and I hope against hope that sooner or later they will abduct us and fly with us through a black hole in time and space into a parallel reality or similar.

One morning, four or five days later, the symptoms miraculously start to die away and our guts rumble in an empty duet. In the hope of solid food, our intestines mark seconds, minutes and hours with the precision of a Swiss watch. Listening to our inner workings, we realise—it is Norberto who comes to the conclusion first of all—that it has been two weeks since the door to the cellar closed, and that we have heard nothing from Dori Galdaretxe; we haven't even heard the wheels of her chair squeaking. This realisation has a devastating effect on our already low morale. My mind, as sticky and vulnerable as a snail that has to hide in its shell, starts to imagine a movie in which we appear with Dori in sequential, parallel scenes. She's on some paradisiacal beach, self-satisfied on top of her inseparable chair, getting a tan and taking gulps from a large grapefruit and mango slushie. We are consuming our own bodies until we turn into those pathetic skeletons that little girls with pigtails or mediums in trances find sitting in the corner of a room in terrible horror movies. Dori's movie is in colour, with a cast of thousands; ours is a home video, fixed shot, in black and white.

The same day we light a fire to warm ourselves with the last match and the last pages of a romantic novel whose author I cannot remember. The last candle went out at dawn, along with a good chunk of our hope; in fact, for some time there have been four of us in the basement: Norberto, the cold, the damp and me. These new tenants don't help the situation very much. Into the stagnant atmosphere with its mixture of smells—excrement, urine, vomit and the abandonment of all bodily hygiene—there now enter huge clouds of vapour whenever one of us breathes, and each morning the walls are spattered with a kind of interior dew, a kind of natural stucco. This is the medium in which we need to take our final decision: to carry on fasting and try to survive for as long as possible on Coke and Lemon Fanta, or to eat human flesh.

The deliberations are difficult, rough and multiple. On one hand, there is the moral dimension: it is not good to eat creatures like yourself. It's not good Christian behaviour. On the other hand, there is the idea of survival: a survivor is someone who survives everything, even survives what it takes to survive. We need to combine two antagonistic points of view, and after three hours debate, trying to find common ground, we reach the conclusion that the only possible way to proceed is with steak. We will try to stay alive, even if we lose our humanity in the process. The decision to eat the flesh of our coevals is made mere seconds before the last fire goes out, which makes things much more complicated, and ties us in culinary knots.

Carpaccio seems to be the ideal solution to our troubles, and it is a revelation. Cut into thin slices and drizzled with a little Lemon Fanta, human flesh—if I may be so bold—is exquisite. All you have to do is get your mind ready, let your imagination run free. To think, for example, that the former owner of this body you are now eating killed his mother with an axe to the head, or raped a junkie in a derelict lot, or ate pasta with his mouth open. Thinking like this almost helps work up an appetite.

At the risk of stating the obvious, the longer a person remains kidnapped, the more annoying his daily life becomes.

Norberto and I can bear witness to this. In barely a fortnight we run out of most of our topics of conversation, and that, sooner or later, brings us into contact with an existential axiom: man is an empty space across which wisdom passes at the speed of light. Daily life, on the other hand, is turning us into pieces of the same mechanism. One of us will start a sentence and the other will finish it, and vice versa; the two of us scratch behind our ears at the same time; and each of us, in a vain attempt not to be discovered jerking off by the other, actually ends up masturbating at the same time underneath the covers. In spite of not actually being alone, sometimes the feeling of solitude is so great that if Luana Varsavsky the university ogre were to join us, then she would be met with passionate kisses. On the mouth.

On 31 March our supplies run out, and as a result the phantom of certain death moves into the basement. It is as if the air in the room, naturally heavy and pestilent, had become one hundred times more dense, and every move that we make, however tiny, forces us to engage with this rotten clinging mass. In the absence of provisions, we can give ourselves the luxury of keeping the freezer doors open all the time. To a certain extent the light that spills out of it is food for the soul, a metaphor for the resurrection. It makes us feel alive, or rather, less dead. Norberto often fantasises about the possibility of closing ourselves in the fridge, one in each compartment, in a foetal position. He has read an article in an American magazine about cryogenics, and doesn't want to miss any possible scientific solution to our problem. All I do is agree with him in everything. Do it, I say, at least that way I'll have fresh meat. In truth, now that I think about it, neither of us is joking.

It is much more easy to deal with being hungry than with being thirsty. On 1 April, early in the morning, after attempting to drink our own urine, we start licking the moisture off the walls. Every drop of water is an incomparable event, a crystalline diamond sliding down our throat. The rest of the day we spend lying on our blankets so as not to waste a single molecule of energy. Norberto says nothing. He keeps looking at the light that comes out of the freezer. He is still looking at the light when he offers me his knife to cut his throat.

'Have you gone mad?'

'No,' he answers, 'but I don't want to.'

His face is that of a man sunk impossibly deep into depression. He has a thick beard and prominent cheekbones. The spotted handkerchief is still tied round his neck; it seems like a souvenir thrown up on a beach and collected by a castaway.

'I don't know,' I say. 'Maybe tomorrow. Try to get some sleep.'

That night, or maybe later the same day, I'm not sure, I have a dream. I am asleep, draped in the filthy blanket, and suddenly I jerk awake and jump easily out of my body. I am still asleep and at the same time I am standing up looking at myself while I sleep. That's it. And my new body, which is the same as my old body in every respect, walks over to the wall while I am sleeping and passes straight through it. The dream is so real that it scares me. It is raining heavily outside, under a full marble-coloured moon, but I don't even get wet. Some sort of magnetic field around my body repels the water, and the rain stays floating in the air, like snow in a snow-globe. There are some bushes in the distance and a halo of light behind them. I walk towards it, but as I approach the light it fades away. When I get there, there is no light, just a metal spoon thrown on the ground, a shitty rusted metal spoon.

It is one of the most ridiculous dreams I have had in my life, so I am sure that it must mean something. Not even in dreams is it possible for there to be such random nonsense. I spend several hours trying to find meaning in this ridiculous image of the spoon. My head transforms it into a catapult, or a kind of metallic lute with the strings stretched across the bowl, or a decoration hanging from the neck of a yellow-eyed Venusian... I am about to give up when my vocal cords suddenly twang and release the name Uri Geller. Norberto, who is trying to get some sleep, suddenly sits up and hands me his knife.

'Here,' he says. 'You need it more than me.'

I pretend not to hear him and remain sunk in my thoughts as the noise of the freezer gets ever louder. Somehow, I reach the conclusion that our imprisonment is a kind of spoon that I have to bend, a sort of spoon made from mental steel that is blocking our exit. Life is nothing apart from an enormous spoon, and our destiny is nothing more than attempt to twist it without touching it. More that this, I think, our experiences are a series of bent spoons that lie in a row behind us. Our first steps, the first day of school, the first fight, the first kiss... Everyone leaves his own row of bent spoons behind him as he goes through life, and if they are not bent enough, bent into a right angle at least, maybe they follow us, clinking, right until our last breath. We are—and here I am referring to humankind in general—made of flesh and water and will, and will is a part of the mind. It is the mind that pulls the strings. Things don't just happen. There is an inner force in all of us that makes them happen.

Immediately, I try to put these new certainties into practice. I concentrate on the wall with the same aggravation as I did years ago, looking at Doña Reme's window. Norberto looks at me for a moment, patronisingly. Then he says that I'm really auditioning very hard for a straitjacket and wraps himself up in his blanket again. To begin with my intention is to open a crack in the wall that will allow us to return to the world, but soon I realise that this is a pretty crude idea. It must be that the wall is full of cracks, invisible wounds that are bored of waiting for someone or something to pass through them. Just as I am trapped in my body, the cracks are trapped in the wall. The solution is to find a common imaginative space, an immaterial space to make contact. The dream universe offered itself as a quick solution. If I could control my own dreams, like a driver in charge of his car, then maybe I could find a crack, or even pull the wall down.

As the days go by, it becomes clear that my theory of the dreams is stupid. On the one hand, it is impossible for me to control them, and in fact I more often than not end up tossed around by them. I am a poor fool stuck in a gale. On the other hand, dreams are parallel to reality, and it is just this state of parallelism that stops them from meeting at a single point.

Over the next few days our physical deterioration means that I am no longer able to pose myself significant metaphysical questions. In fact, as if I were playing a game of Ludo that had ended up taking over my whole life, I am sent back to the beginning. What happens is that in a return to the domestic mentalism of my childhood I spend several hours each day closing my eyes and wishing with all my strength to be taken out of there, while Norberto heads to a borderland between stasis and death. I want so much to escape, that on several occasions, each time more easily, I manage to leave the basement. On these trips, usually short in duration, I sit down with my family after Sunday lunch with a steaming mug of coffee and a tray of pastries in front of me, or else walk along the banks of the Ereaga, or dive into the hubbub of a Saturday night on Licenciado Poza Street. Every fantasy is a discovery, and every discovery is a fantasy.

On the morning of 7 April the doors of the goods lift open and several policemen with machineguns and torches come in. Behind them come two men in casual clothes holding their noses. According to Norberto's watch, it is 08:50 precisely. Looking at the watch is all we can do at this stage. Our bones are numb and we feel that they are as fragile as an old man's neck. We have spent several days defecating on ourselves. The two men in plainclothes start looking around and one of them orders two policemen to get us out of there. Upstairs they lay us out on fold-out beds and some very kind nurses wash us with wet sponges and give us water to drink in very small sips. I want to thank the woman, but I can barely speak in a whisper. Instead of smiling, I must be twisting my face into tragicomic grimaces. Daylight hits my retinas as a series of sparks, balls of painful light, and I can barely make out the faces of the people who are near me except for Norberto's. I can see his face clearly. The situation is more unrealistic than most of my recent dreams.

And then the nurses separate our beds so we are three or four metres apart and one of the plainclothes men who has just come up in the goods lift leans over me. The other one stands at the foot of Norberto's bed. The two of them begin a kind of interrogation. Norberto's interlocutor is a distant sea-blue stain with a pair of legs. Mine is a middle-aged man, dressed in a beige overcoat, whose sole distinguishing feature is a sparse rectangular moustache. He looks sad, a little tearful, like one of those dogs that are abandoned in the summer in an underpass. Inspector Basilio Olabarrieta, which is how he introduces himself to me, says that they found Dori Galdaretxe dead half an hour ago in the house. This news makes my jaw drop. The corpse is outside in the garden, waiting for the arrival of the forensic examiner, but everything suggests that Dori Galdaretxe died weeks ago of a heart attack. I imagine her in her chair, covered in a huge golden thermal blanket, underneath a sort of circus tent set up over the beech tree's uneasy roots, and I suddenly feel very cold. As far as the motive for the kidnapping is concerned, Inspector Basilio can't help me, just suggest a number of disparate and self-evident facts. By now they have taken Norberto into another room. I think it is my duty to tell the Inspector about the hand and the other human remains, and I do. The news seems to send him into an introspective trance. He mentions the name of Gaetano Iabichino, an Italian actor. I insist on more information, and he says that they found him dead years ago in Milan, poisoned. The body was missing a hand. A crime of passion, almost definitely. There were a few clues leading to Dori Galdaretxe, but nothing could be proven. The meat you have eaten must be beef. At this moment, as I hear this, I feel an instantaneous relief, but as the minutes pass I start to feel more and more disappointed. Anthropophagy would have given our survival a certain heroic nature, and now all that we have is two Psychology students trapped with a well-stocked fridge: it is a black and indelible stain on our legend.

I can barely recall the rest of my conversation with the police inspector. When it is over, they take me on the bed through the back door of the house—I suppose they don't want me to see Dori Galdaretxe's corpse—and put me into an ambulance. Norberto is at the top of the ramp on his bed, with the two nurses. Now I can see everything a little more clearly. Norberto looks a lot better, he's so close we can almost touch each other. His face has become pinker, and his voice, although still weak, is masculine. He smiles and puts a hand on my right shoulder. It was the car, he says. The Mercedes. A neighbour saw it abandoned at the roundabout and called the police. That's how they found us. Of course, buddy, I murmur. That's what it was: the car.

2. [Triangle]

The Iabichino Case

The first time I see Dori Galdaretxe is in the second or third segment of a newsreel in the Cine Gayarre. As the winner of one of the national theatre prizes, I can't remember exactly which one, Dori walks across one of the rooms in the El Pardo palace, bows before a vegetative General Franco and, without showing any sign of repulsion—she must be a great actress—kisses his right hand. I am nineteen and my brain is pickled in semen. There's no space for anything else in there. My first and only dream is to become Marlon Brando and grow old smearing butter into young women's anuses. If anyone had told me back then that I would earn my living as a police inspector, I'd have broken his nose. By some kind of perverse engineering, lust has built itself a little projector in the attic of my brain and whenever I close my eyes I can see private lingerie catwalks, stripteases where my friends' mothers take the main roles, and standardised pornographic scenes. My right hand is always so busy that I often feel like I've been born with only one available arm.

Dori Galdaretxe, along with Ursula Andress and Raquel Welch, wins, on merit—to some extent all targets of masturbation are decided on merit—a privileged position on my altar. By contrast with Andress or Welch, La Galdaretxe rejects the cinema. She considers it a diseased medium, capable of making anyone into an actor by the sick repetition of take after take after take. It's for beginners. Amateurs. If we exclude the big screen, then Dori's face can only be found in theatre stalls, boxes, balconies, occasional television appearances—always as a guest—and in glossy magazines. A large percentage of these magazines can be found under my mattress: a series of sticky colour photographs, some of which I still have, although I tear most of them into pieces the morning she marries Gaetano Iabichino, an on-and-off star of Italian theatre, in Milan. That morning, while the wedding march is playing and a rain of petals falls on the happy couple—at least, this is how it happens in my mind—I decide to get rid of her once and for all.

Eight or nine years later Inspector Dino Manzini of Interpol calls me to ask for our help with a murder committed in Milan. A maid has found Gaetano Iabichino floating face down in his own bathtub, his black hair spread over the surface of the bloody water like some new kind of seaweed. The body has had its right hand removed with a single clean blow; however, initial analysis suggests that death was caused by poisoning, the least heroic of crimes. By this time, Dori Galdaretxe and Iabichino are no longer a couple. They have signed the divorce papers—on the same day I recovered the last photographs of Dori from under my mattress—and confirmed the act with scandals and alternating exclusives in the gossip magazines. Gaetano accuses Dori of being cold and distant, cold as a frozen piece of meat. Dori, for her part, calls her husband *il presto*, the fastest man (in certain, not very complimentary senses) on this side of the Atlantic.

On her return to Bilbao, Dori Galdaretxe abandons the stage for good and retires to a little villa in Neguri that belonged to the heirs of the shipping magnate Sota. To begin with one often sees photographers and other curious parties—I include myself among the second group—regularly hanging round the edge of the property looking for an autograph or even a possible appearance of the star herself, but the passage of time, together with the appearance of two scowling Dobermans of unusual ferocity, limited the number of curious people, reducing them in practice to casual passers-by and those who wished to have a melancholy wank. First of all people forgot about Dori; then they forgot that the villa was inhabited, and in the end they forgot that it even existed. The place had become invisible once again, just like the docks, the breakwater or the esplanade, all those places which had never been any different from how they are now, which are both presence and absence, no-places, nothings made of stone.

It is on the evening of 20 July 1981 that I cross the threshold of that particular nothing for the first time, in order to

35

investigate what Inspector Manzini calls *la conexione spagnola dil criminale asunto di Milano*. Dori Galdaretxe keeps me waiting for several minutes outside, in earshot of the menacing barks of the Dobermans, which I never actually see. Later on she tells me, as she pours me a glass of cold water, that as they were barking all through the night and at other inconvenient moments, she has swapped the dogs for a recording. They're both here, on the table, she says, in this cassette. Dori is beautiful, as beautiful as my memory of her, although she is a little drunk. A watery look in her eyes shows that she has allowed Martini hour to stretch until it hits the time for pre-dinner drinks. She slurs her speech a little.

'I didn't have anything to do with all that Gaetano stuff,' she says, as she pours a finger of Cointreau into a tall glass with ice. She has her back to me, wearing a white dress that is very short and shows off her curves, leaning gently against the bar.

Of course, Sam Spade or Marlowe would say something witty when faced with this view—excuse me madam, would you mind showing me the back door, or similar—but I am Basilio Olabarrieta, from the Calle del Perro, right in the heart of Bilbao, and at this precise moment I am concentrating as hard as possible to make sure my fly-buttons don't pop.

'We are aware of that, madam,' I reply. 'It is clear that you could not have been the criminal agent here. Poisoning someone a thousand miles away nowadays, what with the state of the postal service, is practically impossible.'

My hostess pours a little bottle of chocolate milkshake on top of the Cointreau and comes towards me, stirring the mixture the whole time.

'Do you always speak like this?' she asks.

'How?'

She takes a sip of her drink and then sits on a sofa at the other end of the room, in front of a large French window with the curtains wide open. I sit down in front of her, on an oriental-style ottoman, holding my glass of water. The last of the evening sun comes in, long red waves, and it gives a stateless air to the room, with its babel of decoration—Persian rugs, Florence tapestries and carved masks from darkest Africa. The only object here that seems native is an oak dining table for twelve which has the air of being an inheritance.

'The royal "we", I mean,' she says. 'You said "We are aware of that".'

'Oh, that. Force of habit, it's a habit we have in the force. The vice of formality.'

'I understand.' Dori puts the index finger of her right hand between her upper lip and her nose, in the exact spot where a small-time crook, using a knuckleduster, gave me something to remember him by shortly after I joined the force. 'Did you ever think about growing a moustache?'

'Madam,' I say, 'I'm not going to beat around the bush. You are the main suspect in the murder of your ex-husband. Perhaps you did not put the poison in his coffee, or wherever it was, yourself, but it would not be a ridiculous conclusion to think that someone else did it in your stead.' I pause here to take a sip of water, then I pick up the thread of my argument. 'Look. A crime is not a complicated web of independent mechanisms. It is more like a simple two-stroke engine. Round every corner there's a man willing to kill for money, or for a woman, if she's beautiful.' Dori thanks me for the compliment with a wink. 'That is one of the basic rules of criminology. I just want you to know that from now on we will have a starring role in the play that is your life. That we will be behind you every step of the way.'

'Of course,' she says. 'That's how it is.' I am moved to find a degree of expectation in her glassy stare. 'I am sure that a moustache would really suit you. One of those thin ones, a simple pencil moustache. Just a hint of a moustache, you know.'

She takes a long swig of her drink and politely asks me to leave the house. Outside, on the other side of the fence that protects the house and the garden, across the esplanade, the waves are meekly coming in and a group of boys are playing football on the shore. They are quite a way away, a hundred yards, two hundred, but the wind brings me their voices directly. I stop still for a while and watch them. I would give ten years of my life to be able to run to them, to pick up on a pass, shoot, score a goal, and roll on the ground, getting covered in sand like a chicken nugget is covered in breadcrumbs.

Dori Galdaretxe is a feature in my men's diary for a good month. There is always someone prepared to follow her, and this overflow of volunteerism, which in other cases would have been a revelation, is the cause of several sharp discussions. The brawls to win the right to walk a few metres behind the hypnotic hips of *La Galda*, to climb straight up to her windows, are more than the police station in Alameda de Mazarredo can take. The arguments sometimes reach the ears of the respectable people standing on the other side of the window, waiting to renew their I.D. card or get a passport. In the worst case scenario, the noise makes it across the Nervión, just one more dirty cloud like those thrown up by the Euskalduna shipyard, or surreptitiously gets as far as the La Salve bridge, just like a moped slips through the thick morning traffic, or a rowing boat makes it up along the banks of the estuary under the menacing shadows of the cranes.

In any event, we don't find out anything that we don't already know. Dori Galdaretxe's movements are as predictable as those of a novice chess player: daily trips to the hairdresser and the gym, a hangout called *Extreme* where the diva is pampered like an Egyptian empress by a group of professional flatterers stuffed into nylon leggings. Tuesdays and Fridays: compulsive incognito shopping trips to the Corte Inglés department store, concentrating mainly on the women's shoe section. Pedicure and massage at the hands of a chubby Czech woman called Zátopek, like the famous distance runner, Wednesdays. Occasional Saturday parties with flagrant and captivating displays of affection in the garden. The irresponsible life of a woman who is young, beautiful, divorced and rich.

We have not progressed much beyond this initial stage when I receive in my office the order that will allow me to search the interior of Dori Galdaretxe's house with all the force of the law. I have ordered the warrant on several occasions, with a childish insistence, but up until now, one after another, all my requests have been denied. It is a shame to have to say this, but the application of the Law, and in a wider sense, of Justice itself, is not in the least the same for every citizen. In general, entering the private property of an anonymous, unknown citizen requires nothing more than a swift boot to the door. On the other hand, with certain people one must show deference. The more honest the citizen, the easier the boot is to apply and the thinner the door usually is. It's a police axiom, like 'for a disappeared person to stop being disappeared, we need a man or we need a body', or—and this is a saying you hear a lot in the office—'if you ever go a bit too far, better for the victim not to see his bruises.'

At the fag-end of September, with the blessed warrant under one arm and accompanied by three of my best men, I head off to Dori Galdaretxe's villa. Autumn has reached her garden with all its paraphernalia: the branches of the trees are naked and grey; the leaves are piled up in heaps, or else float on the surface of the pond like sinister tongues; the Sun has abandoned the Earth, heading off like some mad star. Although it is her maid's day off, Dori insists on us sitting down to have breakfast with her.

'This isn't one of your little city flats,' she says. 'There's a lot to search here. You'll need your energy.'

And then, paying no attention to my refusals, she starts to squeeze oranges, make wonderful-smelling coffee, and toast bread in a griddle-pan. Each of my men, after his initial disconcertment, spreads his toast with apricot jam, or cream cheese, or virgin olive oil as the mood takes him. By the time we start work it is nearly midday.

The search, as we discuss it that evening in an Italian coffee shop, is one of the most extensive ones I can remember. Jesús Celada, my most loyal subordinate, was a thief before he became a policeman and over the course of the morning he mentally sets aside his uniform and becomes once again *The Skeleton Key*, one of the most effective B&E men that the Basque country has ever contributed to the national crime figures. I did not know him in his prime, but those who did confirmed that he was one-of-a-kind, a sort of water diviner for swag, capable of finding a valuable object in the most unlikely hiding-places. Based on experimental evidence, Jesús Celada has become irrefutable proof of the fact that crime and its supposed opposite are in fact two halves of a whole, two connected patterns of thought, complementary, that act within the same parameters and have a common origin, which is an extremely common theory among criminologists. *The Skeleton Key* had been compelled to join the police force after accidentally knocking up the first-born daughter of Inspector López de Letona, a huge man whose size derived in part from the vast quantity of anger and bile he produced every day.

We have not given ourselves a concrete objective, and this lack of focus to our investigation makes our search extremely difficult, even as it is, from a technical point of view, thanks to Celada's abilities, exemplary. Textbook, in fact. Celada is not one of those guys who goes into a room and turns everything topsy-turvy. No. He is sensitive, and thoughtful. He takes a slow look around himself, as if he were taking photographs of every object that makes up the panorama, then suddenly, with no prior warning, heads for the shade of a tablelamp, or makes a shovel out of one hand to dig the earth out from a flowerpot, puts his fingers into a pot of honey right the way down to the bottom, or spends a quarter of an hour absorbed in contemplation of an empty parcel, tied with a red ribbon.

In spite of Celada's rigour and enthusiasm, we leave off our search half way through the afternoon without having discovered any proofs or even relevant indications. Dori Galdaretxe is as clean as a whistle, and without a stroke of luck it is likely that the case will remain up in the air, and not just a little way up in the air, but so far up in the air that it's like being at the top of a skyscraper, a skyscraper in some distant metropolis. Manzini himself shares my pessimism when I get him up to speed: *Tutti lo que tenemos per ahora es una grande merda*, he says in his macaronic Spanish, and starts to swear at the other end of the line.

The months go by for Dori Galdaretxe. Far from being resolved, the case file on Gaetano Iabichino's murder grows dusty at the bottom of my desk drawer in expectation of soon being filed away permanently. To balance things out, routine police work, an unedifying cluster of arrests and interventions in fights, fills up my diary and seems to be happy there. I suppose you have heard of the idea of the descending spiral of violence, probably from some talking head on the TV or radio. Well, that's nonsense, violence is not a spiral; it's a closed loop. Anyone who has ever patrolled the streets knows that, with only a few exceptions, crime has a seasonal logic of its own.

42

Summer, for example, is fertile ground for sexual impropriety, housebreaking and pyromania. Spring is for crimes of passion and suicide, or a combination of the two. Iabichino was found floating face down in his bath in the middle of June. Up to a certain point, crime is predictable, as predictable as it is inevitable.

One afternoon, as my shift comes to an end, I think that I hear someone shout my name as I am getting ready to cross Gran Vía towards the department stores. The voice is coming from one of those shop windows filled with Christmas decorations, with a shouting crowd in front of it. On the other side of the glass, an inauthentic Father Christmas is sitting in a sled drawn by a pair of stuffed reindeer, waving to the crowd. The crowd responds to this waving by waving its own multi-coloured mittens. One of these permanently waving mittens, or, to be more precise, a bone-coloured leather glove, is waving at me from a distance. It is Dori Galdaretxe.

'Inspector, Inspector,' she calls, with her arm held high. She is luminous. Radiant. I want her never to stop calling me ever. Sometimes happiness (forgive this sudden spark of pedantry) flourishes in the simplest of moments, when a beautiful woman calls to you from a distance, for example. I respond to the salutation with an almost childish excitement and force my way determinedly through the crowd that separates us.

'Hello, how are you?' I say, squeezing her hand, which she holds out to me elegantly, still encased in its ivory-coloured leather glove. I can't find the right way to address her. Dori seems too intimate, almost offensively familiar. Miss Galdaretxe is a little too formal. Using her full name, Adoración, is inappropriate, as she's still a long way from reaching fifty. 'It seems that we see each other now in more favourable circumstances,' I continue. 'If I may be honest, I must admit I really hate searches.'

'Don't worry. You were doing your job. All I ask is that you don't unpot my geraniums the next time. It was a lot of work to get them back in place again.'

'I'm afraid there won't be a next time.'

'Don't be so sure. If you grow that moustache we talked about, there may be a space for you at my next birthday party.'

'One of those thin ones, a simple pencil moustache. Just a hint of a moustache. I remember perfectly.'

'A prodigious memory.'

'Yes, there are some things I cannot forget. Sometimes they bury themselves in my head and I cannot make them leave. It happens quite often, as is happening now with Gaetano Iabichino.'

'It's odd,' Dori says, 'but with me it's quite the opposite. Sometimes I can spend months without thinking of him. The birthday party is in two weeks' time, on the twenty-eighth of December, at eight.'

'That's *El día de los inocentes*.'*

'Yes, don't put that face on, I already told you I was innocent.'

* *El día de los inocentes* is the Spanish equivalent of April Fools' Day. Dori here plays on the word *inocente*, which means both 'naïve, foolish' and 'innocent.' (*Trans.*)

44

'Do I need to bring a present?'

'No. The moustache will be enough. I need to go now,' she says. And then this great sea of femininity departs, drawing a wake of gazes after her right up until the edge of the pavement, where she stops a taxi with her bone-coloured glove and gets into the back seat.

I let a narrow doormat of hair grow to cover the scar on my upper lip, but I wonder whether or not to attend the party right up until the last instant. And so I am a little late. On the one hand, I don't feel like mixing police business with my social life. On the other hand, whether or not I am a policeman I am still a man, a refined version of that masturbating teenager I used to be, the fetishist and fantasist I once was. As for the case, the Gaetano Iabichino crime, the chances of a solution are slight at this time, all leads older than a cave painting. Weighing them up, the arguments against going to the party are thrown up into the air by the arguments in favour, with the same forcefulness with which a sudden flow of blood makes a penis boing to attention.

And so, at around nine o'clock, under heavy rain, I press the bell at the garden gate and am invited by the hostess to cross the threshold. The garden has suffered the outrages of autumn, and the trees as a result look severe, bald and distant, unpleasant, like bouncers at a nightclub. The waters of the pond, by contrast, are flagrantly disordered. The inflow pipe is like a waterfall, and the torrential flood creates constant gouts and bursts of water that soak the ground freely. A good proportion of the resulting mud clings to my shoes, which I dab at with a handful of Kleenex before going into the house. A skeleton, a man dressed in a black body stocking with all 206 bones printed on it in white—I guessed it was a man from its flat stomach—stamps my invitation and *ipso facto*, in full view of the rest of the guests, it becomes clear to me that I had been invited without my knowledge to a terrifying fancy-dress party.

Inside, in a room decorated with spider-webs made from straw, splashes of red paint and dripping candlesticks, are gathered all kinds of diabolical monstrosities—mummies, vampires, werewolves, pustulent zombies, giant insects etcetera—but the most terrifying of all is a middle-aged man of meek aspect wearing a grey suit. He is sitting on the arm of a sofa, sipping sangria from a test-tube and chatting to a couple of female demons, a leather suitcase perched on his lap. Whenever anyone walks past on his way to the free bar next to the sofa, the man bounces to his feet and displays the inscription on his suitcase in such a way as it cannot fail to be seen: Tax Inspector. It is a terrifying vision. I am still recovering from the chill it gives me when Dori Galdaretxe comes looking for me. Her disguise is a black dress torn to shreds, a series of rips and artfully positioned repairs displaying to their best advantage the more mature aspects of her body. It is extremely carefully planned untidiness.

'I see that you finally listened to me,' she says. And then she takes a sip from a glass of what looks like lava. 'The moustache is perfect,' she adds, 'although your costume leaves a little to be desired.'

'Plainclothes policeman,' I say, spinning a full 360 degrees on my heels. 'People should be scared witless.'

'Yes, it is quite horrible, but there's still time to make it better. A little bit of make-up, a bit of talcum and a candle, we could make you a really excellent corpse.'

'I'm sure you could. I've heard that corpses are one of your specialities. I haven't seen your ex-husband's severed hand crawling around here yet.'

Dori opens her mouth to say something, but a chorus of werewolves stop me from hearing whatever it was. When I manage to get close to her, I hear the following:

'So, do you want to be the main attraction at this wake or don't you?'

'Of course,' I say. And then, following Dori's instructions, the lycanthropes carry me away across the room and lay me out on the large oak table which seats twelve. The rest is easy to imagine. Dori covers my face and my hands with huge quantities of talcum powder to give me an even more cadaverous appearance. Then, waving a lit candle over my face, she personally makes sure that the wax falls so as to give me the appearance of scars—she calls them my stigmata—which she then colours in. Finally, my prone body is surrounded by a dozen or so candlesticks, and I am stuck thinking that it's pretty odd they say a corpse is resting in peace because

1. A significant proportion of the talcum powder is stuck in my nose, with the consequent ticklishness that it inspires.

2. The smoke from the candles is like a thick fog in my eyes (Dori insists that I keep them open to make the effect more dramatic).

3. The wax is burning me a little.

4. Every time Dori bends over me to pay her respects, her nipples poke out through the gaps in her dress, and I am forced to make immense efforts of concentration to avoid this ship of death from raising its mast.

5. At one point I am overcome by sleep, and, as I am later told, my snores compete in volume with the howling of the werewolves.

With midnight come and gone, the monsters start leaving the house in dribs and drabs. The cross the dark garden and disappear onto the other side of the iron fence. A couple of minutes later, the noise of an engine is audible, almost overwhelmingly so, and then little by little the noise fades away until it becomes silence. At one a.m. the only people left in the house are the hostess, a couple of mummies who are dear friends of hers, and yours truly, resurrected. The sangria and the lava have run out hours ago, and Dori is talking about frying some entrails and opening a bottle of Rioja, but the rest of us aren't up for it. The evening has entered into its decadent phase and the three of us, the mummies and me, are trying, subtly, to make it to the door. When the time comes to say goodbye, Dori whispers to me:

'Not you. You stay.'

The mummies disappear into the dark holding hands. The sound of an engine. And on top of the oak table, with space for twelve guests, Dori Galdaretxe, *La Galda*, makes love to me among the shreds of her clothing.

The weekend that follows is an athletic prolongation of this recently established connection. Dori turns off the doorbell and unplugs the telephone and we spend seventy-two hours engaged in a festival of sex. I have never entered and exited a woman so often over such a brief period of time, and each new assault is a milestone in my history as a man. Any time and any place are appropriate for our bodies to come together. On New Year's Eve, with the clock striking twelve on the television, I bend over the sofa and give Dori twelve accurate thrusts, pushing her lucky red pants to one side. The next day, with the New Year concert playing in the living room, we play our own symphony on the mattress springs in her bedroom. And at the same moment as a scrawny Finn with an unpronounceable name slips off the end of the ski jump and shoots into the sky, I too reach my own personal bit of heaven. Basilio Olabarrieta will never be Marlon Brando, and he will never grow old smearing butter into young women's anuses, that much is sure, but this is close enough. Few, very few men are lucky enough to sleep with the woman whose sticky photographs they have kept under their mattress in their youth. And this, when the moment of judgement comes, in the account book of life, must register somehow in the make-up of a man.

This weekend is followed by others, less busy in sexual terms, but far from cooling off, our relationship grows more substantial, more committed. Life and chance have turned my mattress over, and Dori is now on top of it rather than underneath, lying here by my side, very unlike an unfeeling photograph on glossy paper. I can run my fingertips over the flesh-and-blood Dori, I can hug her, I can hold myself tight to her to hear her breathing and smell her scent, I can carry out all those types of action that, if the correct chemistry is produced, may, one imagines, carry a man over the border from sex to love. Dori for her part also seems excited, and I write 'seems' and 'excited' because as the years have gone by I know that a man, in his dealings with women and affairs of the heart, should never be sure of anything. In any case the signs—which I trust just as any dedicated police officer would—suggest that our relationship will move on to the next level just as soon as the Gaetano Iabichino case is finally sent to the archives.

And this, the definitive archiving, takes place on the morning of the thirteenth of February, the eve of Valentine's Day. The teletype that arrived in the office with the logo of Interpol and the signature of Inspector Dino Manzini is unequivocal: *FINITO*, in capitals. That same afternoon I go to the jewellery section of one of the department stores—the same one in whose environs I had my first informal encounter with Dori—and purchase an engagement ring. The next morning, before going to the commissary, I head over to Dori's villa with the teletype in one hand and the ring hidden in the other. As soon as Dori appears at the door I offer her the teletype.

'Read this, darling.'

She takes the piece of paper, holds it between her hands for a while and then slowly unrolls it. She has just got up, is tired and yawning, and her ability to respond quickly is almost non-existent. In spite of the cold, and the freezing damp, the idea of inviting me in doesn't even pass through her head. When she has finally finished reading, I say:

'I told you that you were innocent.'

Then I bring my lips close to hers and give her a kiss. She allows me to do this, but without any passion on her part. It is like kissing a bloody steak. For a few seconds, perhaps a minute, I weigh up the idea of leaving the ring for a better occasion, but I end up rejecting the idea. Officially, Dori is innocent, and so free of suspicion. Also, it is Valentine's Day. It is going to take me a lot of effort to find a better day to propose. The only negative aspect is the cold, that freezing and gelatinous devilish dampness, but February begins with an 'F' because it's freezing. So I open my hand and show Dori the ring. I raise it up to her eye level. It is a modest token, pure, almost sober, a fine loop of twenty-four carat gold without an inscription or any engraving. Dori takes it from my hand between finger and thumb, brings her hand quickly to her chest and then, whipping out her arm with particular accuracy, throws it at my face. The ring hits my head, flies across the garden and, like the ring to some small planet struck out of orbit, spins away until it reaches the fence.

'Have you gone crazy or what?'

'You're a pig, Basilio. The case gets archived and you drag your arse over here to give me a ring. What did you want me to do, dance a jig? Are you completely stupid?'

'I thought you'd like it.'

'And what were you going to give me if they hadn't shelved the case? Handcuffs?'

'You're making too much of this, Dori, and you can't afford to be so dramatic in real life.'

'Really. And that's your advice to me, Mister Police Inspector, who make your living by sniffing people's arses. Well you can go back to whatever hole you crawled out of, but take that shitty ring with you before you leave. I want you to take it away before it ruins my whole garden,' she says, pointing with her chin to its probable resting place, some vague spot between the hedge and the fence.

'You're not being fair to me,' I say, 'and you'll regret this.'

'Yes, I'm regretting it already. I thought you were made of a different material, but now I see you're not.'

'You can't throw all this away just because of a silly little ring, Dori,' I beg her. 'Things don't work like that.'

'You're right there. Between you and me, things don't work like that. They just don't work,' she declares before shutting the door in my face.

The ring is covered with dirt. I pick it up, clean it, and take it back to the jeweller's that afternoon. A few days go by before Dori allows me to pick up my personal belongings: a wash-kit, three changes of clothes and a few old press photographs, proof of my long-standing adoration for her, which I showed her one night and which made her laugh until she cried. When I go in, she is lying on the sofa, eating a bowl of vanilla ice-cream in large, rapid spoonfuls. I have never before seen her eat so intensely. I try to approach her, but she puts up a hand between us as a barrier: the palm pointed towards me like a reflecting screen and her fingers widely separated and extended as far as possible. It is clear that she has no intention of speaking to me. So I gather my belongings and, without making any remonstrations, keeping things as calm as possible, head to the door. At the threshold I meet with two stocky men carrying a freezer on their shoulders. I have to take a step backwards to let them pass. Then I leave and go away quickly. I don't see Dori again until ten years later, in the same house, near to the same sofa, but on this occasion we cannot talk either.

3. [TRIANGLE]

THE REYKJAVÍK SYNDROME

AFTER THREE MONTHS RUNNING OVER IN MY HEAD THE IDEA OF going to Reykjavík, it was a single statistic that led me to book myself onto the first flight out: I read that in the last year only five people had been murdered in the whole of Iceland, and my imagination reflexively filled up with men and women, ruddy-cheeked and extremely gullible. Sipping a cup of tea by the fireside, wearing a groove in their pillow, while out through the window the sun sparkles over the smoke-wreathed summit of Esja; in that same moment I saw myself giving them the *coup de grâce* with a poker, or else trying to avoid their uncoordinated and pathetic kicking as they struggled against being asphyxiated.

I don't know if other murderers (perhaps I should write 'psychopathic murderers') ever think about this, but I've always dreamt of a crime sanctuary: a place where the crime level is extremely low and I can give free rein to my impulses.

But before I continue, I should probably get you up to speed about who I am: I am an occasional and selective murderer, which is to say that I only kill during the summer holidays (the rest of the year I am an exemplary citizen of Madrid), and I never kill my fellow countrymen. Even though it might sound slightly pedantic, what interests me about crime are its prolegomena, those moments when the victim, a cloverleaf in his hand, walks across a park, or says goodbye to his children until the evening with a coffee-flavoured kiss, or lifts his leg onto the third step of a flight of stairs in order to pull up his left sock, without in any of these cases being aware that this will be the last time he does so. In these moments, as I appear on the scene and the crime that is to come starts, with an overwhelming clarity, to take shape in my head, I feel very close to God. The rest, the carrying-out of the homicide, is my job, little more than that. Now that I've made this clear, let's go back to Reykjavík.

My first night in the city is terrible: at the bed-and-breakfast where I am staying, a slum with a shared bathroom on the worst part of Hverfisgata, there is in the basement a juddering nightclub, so I do not sleep a wink all night. The electronic hubbub comes in at my ears in concentric circles, like an earthquake spreading from its epicentre, while the midnight sun enters as it pleases through the holes in an old blind. There is an uncertain moment somewhere between four and five in the morning when I want to be one of those brats in redneck America who one day snap and burst into their classroom or the local hamburger joint with daddy's hunting rifle, just to let off some steam.

The situation gets much better in the morning. At their busiest, the streets of Reykjavík hold fewer people than you would find on a wet Sunday in the Retiro, even though this city is an unpolluted place, whereas Madrid's skyline is like an exhibition of incense burners. A lake in the centre of the old town, the Tjörn, is the focal point of the city, so that Reykjavík when seen from an aeroplane looks like a bluish sun, naïve and reflective, from which rays spread off in all directions. Many different types of wildfowl visit the lake, mostly eider ducks, terns and gannets (in this respect it does resemble the pool in the Retiro, except in the case of Madrid it would probably make more sense to speak less specifically of 'birds'). Citizens rest on the benches here, peeking at each other like people in love, with their hair that is at the same time so bright and so brittle, and their freckled faces; taking the weight off their feet and holding hands on the banks of the Tjörn: it is difficult to believe that their ancestors spread terror throughout half of Europe. Of course, at this point we arrive at an impasse, because I suppose that none of these lovebirds in his right mind would ever think that a Spanish tourist who had kicked his shoes off and was curled up into a ball on a park bench could ever be an implacable killer.

I spent the afternoon walking up and down Laugavegur, the main commercial street of the city, although I don't have any coherent recollection of my actions: I know that I ate a pickled pork sandwich at a table outside a bar (in spring and in summer the streets of Reykjavík are filled with tables, where the clients of bars and cafés sit and look at the sky and attempt to absorb every ray the sun offers); I know I regularly felt my shirt pocket under my jacket to check that I still had my little bottle of tetrodotoxin (the lethal venom of the fugu blowfish); I know that a sturdy young woman served me several cups of a coffee that was both watery and piping hot, and that I spent a while looking at the colourful pop-art window display of a shoe shop. However, it is impossible for me to say in detail what happened next, and all the subsequent images I remember come from later at night, with the midnight sun painting the city gold, and the shadows spreading everywhere, like ghosts.

From this twilight moment onwards, my memory starts to work as precisely as a telescope. I see myself in the geothermal steam of the Smoky Bay, half hidden behind a goods container waiting for a victim to present himself. I have not yet decided exactly how the crime will be carried out, but I know I will beat his head against a solid surface: either the side of this container which doubles as my lookout post, or else the cobalt-blue snaking metal bannister which leads down to the ocean. Meanwhile, I make great pains not to expose myself to the sun, which has dipped slowly into the water and is now pulling up again over the horizon; and also to try not to be distracted from my musings by the siren of a cargo ship or the intense smell of hydrogen sulphide filling my nostrils. When the victim appears, preceded by the porous sound of their footsteps, the rest of the world fades out in my vision until it is reduced to the most minimal possible background: a white and distant canvas. Now the footsteps approach to my right. They sound hollow, agile, lively. I hear them grow louder for a few seconds, barely ten or twelve, and then I stop hearing them. There is only the sunlight, an intensifying bronze light that seems to nourish itself on the foul air and the silence. This is it, I tell myself. I leave my hidey-hole and see the victim's back for a moment, which is as long as it takes for the victim to climb onto the bannister and leap into the void. I am not even in a condition to check if it is a man or woman as I look hurriedly into the Atlantic and see the body being swallowed beneath a foam-crested wave.

That night I change my bed-and-breakfast for another quieter one in the extreme north of Hverfisgata, but even so I find it difficult to get to sleep. Lying in my bed, I can't stop going over this incident, the suicide. The reason for my insomnia is not the fact that the crime was not consummated (in fact, on more than one occasion, in case of emergency, I have been forced to leave people badly wounded or even in a coma, without these inconclusive events stopping me from eating or sleeping); what really is annoying is thinking what would have happened if I had got there before the suicide took the plunge; in that case, if I had committed this crime, I would not have been a murderer, but rather an exterminating angel, exactly the opposite of what I intended. This hypothesis, of what might have been, and thinking about how to avoid such situations in the future, kept me awake until nearly dawn (this is only a manner of speaking: as I have told you before, the sun never sets during the Icelandic summer), when at last I surrendered to sleep.

Three or four hours later I am trying to manage a map of the city with one hand while with the other I drag a red suitcase with wheels down an alley past empty boxes of fish. Ymir, the receptionist at my second bed-and-breakfast in Hverfisgata, has been kind enough to underline for me in a free-sheet a half-dozen people who claim to be renting rooms, and I have decided to deploy all my energies in finding somewhere to stay. In fact, I am also looking for a victim, a widow or a widower or perhaps an old married couple that I will be able to murder without any problems; as soon as I am out of the alleyway I find a phone booth, stick in a couple of kronur and make a few phone calls (in English) just to check: I ask how many people live in the house; if there are children or animals or other guests; if it is a block of flats or a private house; if it is a quiet neighbourhood. All the questions criminals normally ask.

The list of possible landlords, after my phone calls, has been cut down to a couple in the Saebraut district, only about three hundred metres from where I am at the moment: Þóra Þorkelsdóttir, a widow and (in her words) 'a bird-lover', and Helgi Sveinbjargarson, a retired lorry driver, who told me insolently, as he coughed and spat, that he made the best skyr (a kind of thick yoghurt normally served with bilberries and cream) in the whole of Reykjavík.

(As I am aware that Icelandic names tend to generate a certain degree of curiosity, I will try to explain their complications here. They are in fact very simple to form. In most cases you take the genitive of the father's name, and then add the ending –son [for a boy] and –dóttir [for a girl]. Names generated from the mother's name are also legally permissible. And now—practically no one can resist—you work out what your surname would be by the Icelandic method.)

Saebraut still has an air of provincial seaside town about it, with its low-slung buildings and its bright coloured houses and its bicycles, which drive by on both sides of a bed of bougainvillea planted in the middle of the road. It is something people say a lot, that there are places where time seems to have paused; in Saebraut, time has not just paused, but has decided to stay still for ever; if it were not for the smoking vents emerging chaotically from the seashore, then you would think that you were trapped in a photograph, or worse still, a postcard.

When Þóra Þorkelsdóttir appears slowly at the door of her house, a sweet little two-storey lime green building, my first impression is that she deserves to die: she is almost deaf, and I think that this must be the reason why she can live with dozens, maybe hundreds of birds. A whole rosary of metal cages hangs from the beams in the roof, and from the walls of the rooms: there is scarcely space left to hammer a nail, and while Mrs Þorkelsdóttir shows me the ground floor, door after door, room after room, the background noise grows more and more deafening. Luckily, the first floor, which you reach via a spiral staircase, is much more tranquil. The two bedrooms are there, one facing another, Mrs Þorkelsdóttir's room and the guest bedroom. There is also a bathroom, a separate toilet and a small living room with a modest collection of books and a portable television. The portraits of Þora attract one's attention (Mrs Þorkelsdóttir has told me by now several times, in her simple English, almost shouting, to call me by her first name, so I shall obey her wishes), as do those of a man, who must almost certainly have been her husband. They are photos of day-to-day living (no birthdays or weddings or anniversaries), and there are almost as many of them as there are cages on the ground floor, and none of them show the couple together. In one of them, the one that hangs in the centre of the far wall, over the television, a younger Þora hangs a red dress on a washing line; in another one, her hair tied back in a pony-tail, she is turning over a piece of salmon in a butter-smeared frying-pan. As for the man, with his gigantic hands and his thick moustache, he is cutting at a Chinese rose-bush with some pruning shears, or else pours seed into one of the feeding-trays in a cage, or even raises a mug of beer to his lips, hidden as they are under his foam-stained moustache.

I like the guest bedroom: the bed seems soft and the furniture (wardrobe, washstand, table and wooden valet), even though simple, fulfils its purpose admirably. Also, the blind functions well and does not allow a single ray of light to pass through when it is shut. When I agree to stay, Þora asks me to let her see my passport, and I whip it out straight away. *Madrid*, she screams, *very nice. Very*, I yell. And as soon as she gets out of my sight, I shut the door, take off my clothes, hide the bottle of tetrodotoxin under the pillow, and lie down on the bed to plan the crime.

And I am naked and recovering from the smell of rotten eggs that came along with the sulphurous water of the shower when I hear someone knocking heavily at the door of the bathroom. I dry myself, and with the wet towel wrapped round my waist, I hide behind the door and open it halfway. On the other side, a little pale and disturbed, Þora asks me at the top of her voice to help her unload some boxes that she has just brought from the supermarket. I accept, and we agree that I will come down and meet her at the garage door in ten minutes, round the back of the house. As I tie my shoelaces, I go back over the previous scene and think that I have just missed an excellent opportunity: I could have opened the door completely, let my towel drop to the floor and, in the face of Þora's natural surprise, thrown myself on her neck and stifled her last shouted words. But I am not efficient when it comes to improvisation, I have never been so in the past and I don't think that I will manage to be so in the future. Every crime needs its own tools, and once it's been planned down to the last detail, it is better not to change the course or order of events.

The birds seem to sense my presence, and they scream ever louder as I walk along the ground-floor corridor to the front door. Animals can sense danger or even death. Once, when I was relaxing in a bar in the Quartier Latin in Paris, a girl sitting at a table nearby was holding a German shepherd puppy in her lap. The dog did not stop growling at me for the whole half hour that I was sitting at the table. I know that dogs growl and bark (it would be hard to expect them to do anything else), but there were more than twenty people in the bar and the dog had its eyes fixed on me the whole time as it growled. What is more, as soon as I got up, the beast leapt from the girl's arms, and if it had not been on a leash then I am sure it would have attacked me. Two weeks later, on a very hot night, I killed a poor old man on the Champs Elysées: I bashed his head in with a rock as he was bending over a drinking fountain. A few days later I saw the funeral on television: when I saw the little girl (this time without her dog) throwing herself on the coffin, my blood froze.

The boot of Þora's car, an old, dark red Mercedes, is filled with bags, boxes and skilfully wrapped packages; most of them contain tinned food and jars of vegetables, but there are a few boxes of beer and several bottles of rosé wine. Þora's idea was for me to help her carry the heaviest packages through to the kitchen. Once there, she would unpack them into the cupboards and the fridge. In preparation for this, she has put on a pair of denim dungarees and has tied her hair back in a pony-tail, exactly as in the salmon-frying picture, although it is more than obvious that several years have gone past since the first picture was taken. If she and her husband, with the moustache, had ever had a child (the absence of photos leads me to suggest that they did not), I calculate that he would now be more or less my age.

You can hear the birds from the garage, but the noise becomes unbearable as I enter the house with the first packages in my arms. They are small, bright-coloured birds, the sort that would fit into a fist, and they are maddeningly active: not one single second goes by when they don't stick their beaks up into the air, spread their wings, spin round or try to jump on the bars of the cage, and all the time they don't stop making noise. I leave the packages on the kitchen table and get out as fast as I can. When I am back in the garage I think I hear Þora calling my name, but I don't see her. The bedlam of the caged birds does not allow me to hear where Þora's voice is coming from, and it is now little more than a whisper. In the end I find her face up on the ground, next to the car; a trickle of vomit is running down her chin, her breath comes with difficulty and, in a kind of macabre choreography, she lifts up her hands and puts them to her breast, to her neck and to her jaw before she, with almost no strength left, grabs hold of mine. A minute later she loses consciousness and I stay next to her body, on my knees, with the noise of the birds filling my head; some neighbours come by and I hear in the distance a male voice calling for an ambulance. Scarcely a quarter of an hour later, a young and willowy doctor puts his right hand to Þora's left wrist, then tries to find a pulse in the carotid artery, and then, with a severe expression on his face, certifies her death, from a heart attack. Then I go into the house and open all the windows and all the cages, quickly gather my little bottle and my suitcase and head off in a bad mood, leaving peaceful Saebraut behind me as the birds fly off to their certain death.

My first plan is to go to find Helgi Sveinbjargarson, the retiree who says that he makes the best skyr in the city. However, this plan only runs around my head for a few seconds, and then it flies away, like Þora Þorkelsdóttir's damn birds: the old man's health could give out at any moment, and I wouldn't like to have his last bloody phlegm spattering my shirt. Also, after these two frustrated attempts, I am feeling tired and lacking in confidence, to the extent that I would find it difficult to crush a bug under the sole of my shoe. I need six or seven hours of uninterrupted sleep and also something to take my mind off things: a proper hotel and maybe a daytrip. After all, I am on holiday, and I won't get any more time off for several months.

The Skjalbreid, a four-star hotel at number 16 Laugavegur, the shopping street I walked up and down on my first day in the city, seems to me a definite option. It is one of the most elegant buildings in the whole of Reykjavík, formerly a rich family's town house. For the first time since my arrival, everything goes according to the script, and after a plate of dill-marinated gravlax, a bubble-bath with not a single whiff of sulphur to it, and eight hours of deep and uninterrupted sleep, I find myself in the lobby, sitting in front of Bjarni, a smooth-faced tour operator who sits at a Perspex table and offers me a tour to the south of the island. The tour, he announces, consists of a selection of lava-fields, geysers, boiling waterspouts and volcanoes both extinct and active; it is an offer, he insists, which it would be crazy to refuse. He also offers me the possibility of choosing between an English-speaking and a Spanish-speaking guide; in the second case, the group will consist of only the guide (his own sister) and myself, and consequently the price will be a little higher. I pretend that I am thinking about it, and then after a few seconds scribble an illegible signature on a yellow receipt, hold out a wodge of kronur, and shake his hand vigorously. My palm still warm, as I get up from the chair, I can't stop myself from experiencing a vision of the kid picking up the phone and hearing a neutral voice, perhaps the voice of a police officer, tell him that they have just found his sister murdered. I can hear how Bjarni's voice dies away into nothing and how the leather of the chair creaks as he collapses into it, and I see the handset falling away and hanging suspended a couple of centimetres above the soft carpet. The scene, which starts to run in a loop in my mind, brings me nothing but pleasure, consolation, a sickly kind of wellbeing, only improved upon by the act of contemplating the smile which the sale has brought to Bjarni's face; a smile which will disappear, perhaps forever, when he is provided with the evidence that he is as guilty as the murderer because, in some way, even some involuntary way, he has been connected with his sister's demise.

Finna, Bjarni's sister, meets me the next morning in a black ATV whose body and wheels seem to have received a sparse but obstinate dousing in ash and mud. She is a thin thirty-year-old, fragile-looking, but when I see how easily she picks up my red suitcase, in spite of my gentlemanly demurrals, and throws it in the boot, then I have no choice but to change my opinion. I will not be so strong when I have to throw her body into a pit (especially if I have to dig the pit first), but this would be to anticipate events, because I have still not decided on the details of the crime, and even less how I am to get rid of the body.

It only takes a few minutes for us to get out of the centre of Reykjavík, and as soon as the last suburban buildings are behind us, with our backs now to the ocean and the black sand beaches, on both sides of the road there extends an idyllic landscape of valleys, lakes and geothermal plains. Finna is not very talkative, and while she drives her only concessions are made with her right hand, which she raises from the steering wheel every now and then in order to point with her black-painted fingernails to a geyser, or else to turn up the radio, with its convulsive mass of shouting, guitars and drum solos. It is clear that if I want to win her confidence, I will have to work harder.

'Where did you learn to speak Spanish so well?' I ask. In fact this is a trick question, because up until this point the only words that have come from her mouth have been a greeting and a few basic instructions about the trip, but these have all been delivered in extremely respectable Castilian.

'In Logroño,' she replies after turning down the radio. 'I had a husband who was a footballer who played there for ten years.'

'He played for Logroñés?'

'Yes, if you like football, maybe you remember him. He was called Einarr Olafson,' she explains while, to our left, steam comes out of the crater of a volcano.

'Olafson, a good striker, but you said "was". Did he die?'

'Only to me: I caught him cheating on me.'

'Well, I don't want it to seem that I'm trying to apologise for him, Finna, but elite footballers are surrounded by temptations. It's enough to go to a training session to see the number of willing girls who hang around them.'

'Don't go there... I found him in bed with a student journalist. He had the guy's cock in his mouth and when I opened the bedroom door he nearly swallowed it.' Suddenly, Finna bursts out laughing. She laughs so whole-heartedly that after a few seconds I am caught up by it. When we are both calm, she adds, 'You should have seen it.' Then she shuts her mouth and puffs out her cheeks as if she were a blowfish and

68

starts to laugh again as she puts her foot down and turns the volume on the radio back up.

At midday we reach Geysir, a tourist spot that is a hub for travellers. The plan is to settle down into a log cabin away from the hubbub, to buy some food in a store and then start walking round the lake, Þingvallavatn. The North Shore, which we reach after a strenuous two-hour walk, offers great views of the continental rift that separates Europe from America (a clean vertical cut in the bittersweet cake that is the Earth). To Finna, even though this is the thousandth time she has seen it, it seems a fascinating spot, just as it must seem to the dozens of tourists who, a few metres further on, taking advantage of a bend in the path, make admiring faces and take photos.

'What do you think?'

'I don't know,' I say as I wipe the sweat off my forehead. 'It's beautiful, but slightly upsetting at the same time.'

'Upsetting?'

'Yes. The ground is splitting, it breaks, and there's nothing anyone can do to stop it.' Finna looks at me in surprise with her pale, washed-out blue eyes, and pulls the hair off the back of her neck. 'In thousands of years,' I continue, 'the world will be broken up like a biscuit in a glass of milk.'

'Most likely,' she smiles. 'But we won't be here to see it...'

'No. And that's the beautiful part.'

The way back, past waterfalls, rivers and little lakes, is the most pleasant. The sun is beating down on us, but the closeness of the water has a refreshing effect. Finna is an expert hiker, but it doesn't seem to bother her to adjust her pace to mine, which is slower and less secure. As we wade across a river, with our boots hanging round our necks, she tells me that the first time she went out camping with the Scouts, when she was five, it was difficult for her not to wet the bed, and so her mother put several pairs of plastic pants in her rucksack. Then, without adding any further commentary, she falls silent, as if she is away in some other world, and her cheeks redden. Finna is strange: she openly talks about Olafson the cocksucker, and then an innocent anecdote makes her feel ashamed. It's as if she could guess at my daydreams, as if she knew that by hearing her story I had seen and smelt her cunt, that I had seen it grow up, get covered in hair, become wetter and more welcoming, that my tongue had investigated every fold and had rummaged in each hidden corner of her intimate parts. And this, the possibility that she can walk in and out of the labyrinths of my mind, excites me and disturbs me at the same time.

That night, I decide to invite her to eat with me. While she, wrapped in a dressing gown, wafts her hair around with a portable dryer (the door to the bathroom is half open so that the mirror doesn't get steamed up), I try to get the fire woken again and rummage around in the fireplace with a heavy poker. In the south the temperature goes down several degrees during the night, and so it is sensible to have the cabin heated in our absence. Meanwhile, Finna has come out of the bathroom for a moment to get some jeans and a black t-shirt from her bag, and with the clothes in one hand, has gone back into the bathroom and shut the door. You can no longer hear the motor of the hairdryer and so the noise of the flames is audible; their red crests rise and fall spasmodically. While I wait for her I look out of the cabin's only window: it shows a distant horizon of steam and volcanoes which shine metallically in the light of the sun.

The only decent restaurant anywhere near Geysir is the Trattoria Venezia, or so Finna tells me as she takes the key out of the door of the ATV, which is still covered in ash and mud. As we go through the glass door into the restaurant, Luigi, the owner, throws himself on her and gives her a scandalous kiss on the forehead. *Mia cara ragazza*, he says, delicately holding her wrists. He says a lot of other things as well, but this is all that I catch in the flow of Italian—and occasionally Icelandic—words that pour out of his mouth. Finna reveals to me that, before signing for Logroñés, Einarr played a few seasons in Brescia, which is how come she speaks a little Italian. 'You know, Einarr had ants in his pants,' she whispers, and then smiles, a smile which Luigi takes as being meant for him before he turns and guides us to a table at the back.

Although it has only just gone seven, around thirty people completely fill the dining area. Most of them are starving tourists who take huge bites out of soft triangles of pizza or who suck in smoking plates of spaghetti by the light of three candles (one green, one red and one white, all of them on the tables in a strict approximation to the colours of the Italian flag).

Seeing people eat, chewing and slobbering over their food until it is reduced to a uniform pulpy paste, is something that wakes my killer instinct, and if Finna were not with me then it is very likely that I would choose a single victim from among those present: this fat woman with napolitana sauce on her chin who crosses the room in front of us and disappears suddenly behind a screen; or, better yet, this toothless old man who looks at Finna and me sidelong and then slides his spoon slowly into a creamy serving of tiramisu. I would follow his car with the ATV, and then, after passing it, I would stop a kilometre or two ahead, parked on a bend with the hazard warning lights turned on. It is very likely, almost certain, that upon seeing me in a spot of trouble, the old man would stop to help me. In this case, by some kind of trick, I would make him lean into the space between the open door and my seat. Once he was positioned, I would break his face with the door, would slam it again and again on his bloody head until he collapsed.

'Is that all you're going to eat?' 'That' is a caprese salad, which Finna points at with one of her black-lacquered fingernails.

'Yes, I'm not hungry,' I say, and after instinctively slipping a hand into my shirt pocket, I push a piece of mozzarella up onto the edge of the plate, apart from the rest of the salad. 'But you go ahead, eat...'

'The tagliatelle are excellent,' she says as, with a very precise rotary movement, she pucks several up on her fork. 'You should try them.'

'Maybe tomorrow...' The smoke from one of the candles, the white one, annoys me, and I push it away from me: instead of the Italian flag, the Portuguese one. Then I fill Finna's glass and my own with sparkling rosé wine.

'It won't be possible tomorrow, we'll be getting back to Reykjavík,' she says.

'Maybe on some other occasion, then.'

Finna puts her fork down for a moment and shifts her Siberian blue gaze to a side wall, where hang some black and white photographs of gondolas navigating the Venetian canals. If I am right, and she is able to see my fantasies (the flush which has just come into her cheeks suggests something along these lines), it is possible that she is feeling my cock sliding down her stomach in a straight line until it reaches the gap between her thighs, and how these, wet and warm, are slowly opening, very slowly, almost hesitantly, before her cunt welcomes me in.

'So, are you thinking of staying much longer in Iceland?' she asks, still a little red.

'I'm leaving the day after tomorrow.'

'In that case,' she says, 'we need to drink a toast to your last two days.' Then she lifts her glass and brings it forward, holding it in intermediate space, above the red and the green candle. 'Cheers,' she murmurs.

'Cheers,' I repeat, and move my glass towards hers.

The ATV goes straight past the turnoff to the cabin, and before I say anything, Finna says that she wants to give me a surprise. A few hundred metres further on, we turn off to the left and, after skirting the thick metallic wire fence that marks the edge of a cattle farm, we drive along a rocky road to a flat and sandy expanse.

'Here we are,' Finna says, putting on the handbrake and dropping the car-key into her pocket. 'Wait and you'll see,' she adds.

We wait for a couple of minutes, two or three, in silence inside the car, until suddenly a column of boiling water about twenty or thirty metres high shoots out of the bowels of the earth.

'This is Strokkur, the pride of all the geysers round here,' she explains, and when the spout dies down, another similarly sized one shoots up. 'Well,' she says, 'it looks like we're in luck. You have to see this from close up, but don't get too far away from me. It could be dangerous.'

She opens the door and gets out. I do the same and follow her very slowly, a few paces behind. Once the sandy stretch comes to an end, the ground underfoot, a wet and uneven expanse of old lava, with some lichen growing on it, becomes extremely slippery, and I'm worried with each step that I'll fall and crack my head. When Finna stops with her back to me, I stop too and look at her. Her silhouette, vivid against the water vapour and the midnight sun, is insignificant if you compare her to the latest pillar of water and spray that leaps up into the heavens. I had not planned it like this, but at times the correct moment occurs, and this is not something that you could call improvisation. Whatever you call it, I approach her from behind and put my hands round her neck. Finna tries to give this scene an air of naturalness: she does not get angry with me for taking this liberty, neither does she say anything or make any gesticulations, but I do notice a certain tension in her neck, a knot, small but very tight, and I feel at my fingertips the blood flowing through her carotid artery. If she really knew what I was thinking, then she would turn round. And that is exactly what she does. She turns to me delicately, careful not to break the circle which my hands form round her neck; then, trembling slightly, she lifts her chin and looks at me with her washed-out blue eyes. At this point, all I have to do is kiss her.

For the next two days, until it is time for my flight to leave, we are either in the cabin or in Finna's house, in Reykjavík. There are no geysers, no volcanoes, no thermal vents, no black sand beaches which are worth the bother; time is running out and all we are interested in is kissing each other, letting our bodies intertwine, licking each other, fucking. For these few hours I am not aware that I am about to leave the city without committing the crimes that led me to undertake this trip. I live each moment as if it formed part of a clockwork mechanism of whose engineering I am completely ignorant. It is later, when I am fastening my seatbelt, and the plane is setting off for Milan (where I will transfer onto a flight to Barajas) and the landscape below me is reduced to a rocky grey miniature, that my lack of skill (or luck) is starting to take its toll. But then, sitting to one side of me, a new figure starts to become a protagonist in the tale, as he interrupts each and every one of my thoughts with his pompous voice and his perfect laugh, which is made out of teeth and lip movements that seem to have been made to order. He says he is called Gaetano Iabichnio, and, while he gesticulates with his large and hairy hands, he tells me that he has just appeared, to the great acclaim of both critics and the public—or so he assures me, in spite of my unfeigned lack of interest—in *Macbeth* in the Reykjavík City Theatre. Now he is going back to his hometown, Milan, and then to London, where he will be the lead in *A Streetcar Named Desire*. I am unable to escape from his megalomaniacal ranting until a freckly stewardess, with whom the *artiste* flirts shamelessly, gives us each our trays of food. But it is at this very moment, when escaping from the narrow chairs becomes even more complicated, that he asks me to let him out so that he can go to the bathroom. When I sit back down, after standing in the aisle for a moment to let him get past, I realise that his tray of food is still on the blue tray, and aside from the tinfoil and the plastic cutlery, what I see is a glass filled to the brim with wine, which seems to get bigger with every moment, as if it had been put under a magnifying glass. I put my hand to my shirt pocket in a reflex action and check that the little bottle is still there. All I need to do is turn the cap, pull out the stopper and pour the liquid in without anyone seeing me: paralysis and death in less than six hours.

4. [TRIANGLE]

THE SINCERITY LEAGUE

LIFE, AS I UNDERSTAND IT, ACCORDING TO NORBERTO FRAILE: it is a series of performances: some are star roles and some are minor parts. The bad part is that we can't tell which is which and often we feel that we are the protagonists of a story in which we have actually only been given a couple of lines, or else, vice-versa, we hide our protagonism among the chorus while the centre stage remains illuminated and empty.

Ever since I have had the use of my reason I have loved the theatre. I would claim that I am a creature with theatrical instincts, although in fact we almost all are. We come into the world and almost immediately we discover the immense possibilities offered by crying and try to use them to our own advantage. We cry because we are hungry, because we are thirsty, because we are sick; we also cry to make someone shelter us, caress us, take us in their arms. The rest of our lives—forgive me for this strange synthesis—is just a learning process, substituting this basic crying for other methods of demanding attention: empathy, beauty, seduction etcetera. This latter period of study is, of course, frustrating, almost fruitless, because most of us never find again anything as convincing as this first infantile yell.

Her name is Valle, and I love her, even though that sounds like the chorus to a song. I remember the ticklish feeling I felt in my guts when I saw her for the first time; the short circuit in my brain; the sensation that, without her, my life would turn to grit and stone. This sensation takes place next to the hologram of a fire that is the key attraction in *The Discovery of Fire*, an exhibit in the Bilbao Archeological Museum. There are other people watching the fire, a whole school group, but the only person I see is her.

A high-class filmmaker would shoot this scene in slow motion. Valle's light chestnut fringe would acquire a red tinge from the optical illusion of the flames. Possibly, the crackle of the fire would be heard for a moment over the room's loudspeakers. Valle would, of course, turn towards me with a wide smile and then the camera would dissolve from her mouth to a close-up of my eyes, with the reflection of the flames flickering in them.

But life is not cinema, it is theatre, as I have already said, and in the theatre things happen differently. In fact, Valle does not look at me or at anyone. She looks at the fire and, If I may speak honestly, I don't think she's even looking at that in particular, I think her eyes are looking through it as happens with all adolescents when they are seeing things they find indifferent: the past, mothers and above all boys like me, whose names do not deserve to be drawn inside a heart sketched on an exercise book.

It takes me almost two weeks to speak to Valle for the first time. Every afternoon, my face hidden behind a newspaper, I position myself in front of the metal gate to her school and wait for the bell to ring. I usually sit on a bench in the small park there and pretend to be reading by the light of a streetlamp. Valle is one of the first to leave and this means I have to pay close attention, because sometimes she walks by me so quickly that it is all I can do to catch a quick glimpse of her before she disappears down the street between two towers of yellowish brick. This may seem ridiculous, but at the time to which I am referring it is enough for me to catch a flickering glimpse of her to keep my spirits up.

One day at the end of February, Valle leaves before the bell rings and heads towards the park. It is raining heavily and I have put the classified ads on my head to protect me from the rain. I look like a herring wrapped in wet paper; by contrast, the princess of the discovery of fire takes large strides underneath a comfortable red umbrella. This is a long way away from the type of meeting I imagined, so I do all that I can to turn the situation to my advantage: I pray, or rather mutter to myself. While the drops slide down the eaves of my paper roof, I mutter my wish for Valle to walk past; I desire her to continue walking with the same intensity that I have desired her to stop until this very afternoon. But no one hears me—maybe the rain makes too much noise as it falls—and she stops in front of me underneath her red umbrella.

'Could you lend me your paper for a second? I want to see the film times.'

'Of course,' I reply. Two trickling drops slide down my cheeks.

'It would be better for you to come here,' she says. And then she makes space for me under her umbrella. If I were ever tempted to rank the most marvellous places I have been in my life, then I think that under this umbrella would be at the top of the list. The whole universe could have blown up at that moment and I would not have seen a single flying fragment.

The rain starts to ease off and the air is filled with a pleasant smell of wet ink and damp earth. Meanwhile, we both turn over a few pages until we hit upon the film times. The pink-painted nail of Valle's left hand goes up and down the column twice before hitting on the Coliseo cinema, where they are showing *Gremlins*.

'*Gremlins*, at seven thirty,' she says with a smile. 'Do you do this often?'

'What?'

'Sit on a bench in the rain.'

'No,' I reply. 'Normally I sit on benches when it is not raining.'

'Clever boy. Hey, do you want me to walk you somewhere?'

'No.' I walk out from under the umbrella. 'It's not really raining any more.'

'My name's Valle,' she says.

'Mine isn't,' I answer. And then I turn one hundred and eighty degrees and start to walk away quickly, like a duellist marking his ground, wondering if 'Valle' will be name enough for the both of us.

Scenes like this are repeated over the next few weeks. Valle gets into the habit of sitting with me for a few minutes when she leaves school and we take this opportunity to look at the film listings or scandalous news story (our favourites are crimes of passion or of revenge) under the streetlamp. For various playful reasons I refuse to reveal my identity, and she calls me GB (I find out much later that these initials stand for Guy on the Bench).

In a film—I swear—this flirtation would be shown in an elliptic fashion. I suppose we would be sitting on the bench, next to each other, with the paper spread out over our laps. The surroundings would be the only thing to change, although it is possible that the distance between us would reduce a little as well. The shots could be as follows: a pile of dead leaves at one end of the bench in the first one; maybe a pool of iridescent water; maybe a crescent moon in the background of another. As far as clothing is concerned, the spectator would see a colourful catwalk of hats, jackets, gloves, scarves and tights. The possibilities would be almost endless: but I have already told you—and I stand by my word—that life is not cinema, but rather theatre. And in the theatre actors yawn and doze, they shiver and, if they are adolescents, they suffer from acne.

We move from the park bench to the stalls at the El Carmelo cinema one Sunday morning. The ticket-seller is short sighted and it is hard for me to insist that he sell me two adjacent seats. They are showing *Planet of the Apes*, and while a gorilla on horseback throws a net over a girl, I start to come up with a strategy for my own bit of fishing. I am still working out the last details when I get a kiss from Valle, scarcely more than a slight wet brush across my lips, but enough to tie me to the rails, to offer myself up in sacrifice to the engine of desire. So, having exchanged a few kisses, while Charlton Heston bids symbolic farewell to Liberty on a deserted beach, I bid farewell to my own version as well.

I will sum up the traditional details of our later relationship so as not to stretch this story out too far: my fingertips discover her nipples and vice-versa; her hand strays between my legs and vice-versa; we find ourselves alone in a room and from that moment on we are not the same, etcetera. In the end—I suppose this is a general opinion—there have not been great developments in the field of love since Adam and Eve.

One June afternoon, upon coming out of school, Valle takes me to the door of an abandoned office on the ground floor of a block of flats. It is a dark place, and in contrast to the light outside, that effusive brightness of early summer, it seems impenetrably black: a typical shadowy ecosystem. Wait for me here. I won't be long, she says before sliding through a window that must have had the glass knocked out five or ten years back at least. My first impulse is to follow her, but when I hear the first noise of crunching under my feet, an agonising series of dry sounds, my courage runs out. It was not for no reason that I slept with a nightlight between the ages of three and ten, and although I have tried to fill with adult reasoning this void that my childish fear of the dark produces in me, my fear has still not dissipated (and I don't believe it ever will).

Valle walks three or four metres into the darkness, knocks on a door with her knuckles and then recites enthusiastically, as if singing:

'Milk and sugar, nuts and chocolate...'

'Praliiine!' a male voice says from the other side of the door. Ten seconds later a head sticks out of the window:

'Is this him?' the head says, indicating me with its prominent chin. My eyes are starting to accustom to the edge of the darkness and although it is difficult and a little out of focus, I can see him: a round-faced lad with slanted eyes, about eighteen or nineteen, although you never can tell with round faces. He could easily pass for a citizen of Outer Mongolia.

'Yes, this is him,' Valle replies.

'Well, tell him to come in.'

I go through the window and get in with Valle giving me a helping hand. In the office, a cramped cubicle lit by a pair of candles, there are two other people apart from the round-faced guy, one of them sitting in front of an old typewriter, an Olivetti Lettera, if my memory doesn't play me false. After a prolonged and uncomfortable silence, Valle makes the introductions.

'This tall guy is Monday, and this is his girlfriend, Tuesday. You know Wednesday already; he's the one who opened the door. You will be Friday. As for me, while we're in here, you will call me Thursday. Any questions?' I shake everyone's hand,

83

Wednesday's last of all. The chiaroscuro of the candles makes everyone's face harden, even Valle's; they seem to be wearing masks. In the middle of all this carnival, I feel the urge to run away.

'Friday, great,' I say. And what are we doing here?'

'Everything in its proper time,' Monday says, getting to his feet. He is about the same height as the office.

'Sincerity,' Tuesday says. Monday curls his upper lip and sits down at the typewriter once again. His girlfriend looks at him for a moment, then she fixes her fringe back to her right temple with a clip that seems to appear suddenly in her mouth, and then she starts talking again. 'You are here because Thursday trusts you and we need new recruits for the league.'

I imagine that someone, probably Thursday (Valle) will now tell me what all this cloak-and-dagger stuff about the League is, but no one says anything. Then I hear a buzzing noise. An out-of-tune nimbus of mosquitoes flies over my head towards the candles. Once they get there they stop, suspended around the flames, forming a luminous galaxy filled with an infinitude of craters, a bright misshapen floating Gruyère.

'Straightforwardness, truthfulness, a way of expressing oneself free of falsehoods,' I hear a male voice say, stuttering badly, particularly on the word 'way', where he gets stuck, and on the 'f' of 'straightforwardness', where he has to try three or four times and ends up doing a creditable impression of Daffy Duck. The stammer, I realise, once the mosquitoes are out of the way, belongs to Wednesday, the round-cheeked one, who so far has said nothing more than 'Praliiine' and a couple of simple sentences.

'If that's all you want to tell me...'

'No, it's just the start,' Thursday (or Valle) says. 'The League is much more than this.' At this moment, with the speech just about to get interesting, she picks up one of the candlesticks and, while the mosquito satellite beats a retreat, holds it out towards me. For a moment, my memory dredges up those women from Hammer horror movies who, a candlestick in one hand, a stake in the other, and nipples erect under a camisole, head towards the vampire's coffin with the straightforward idea of stabbing him through the heart. 'The League is...'

'Enough beating around the bush,' Tuesday says, and takes a Polaroid photograph out of her trouser pocket, and holds it out to me. 'This guy in the photo is Heliberto Sagredo, he's thirty-five and lives in my block of flats, just above the carpenter's shop. He got fired about a month ago, they diagnosed him with diabetes last week; yesterday his wife and children left him. And do you know why?' I shake my head. 'Because he's a fat fuck.' I look at the photo again. 'And do you know why he's so fat?' I'm about to give an obvious answer, but I hold myself back. 'Because no one tells him often enough. That's what we do, we tell people about their defects, offend them as often as it takes until they have no other option than to mend their ways. And now, do you want to join us or not?'

I take a sidelong glance at Valle and I see a peculiarly feminine wrinkle in her forehead, a gesture that could be translated as 'Of course, you are free to do whatever you want, but if you don't do what I want you to do, then watch out.' I am sure that Boabdil saw something similar just before handing over the keys to Granada to Ferdinand and Isabella; it's possible that the last thing Brutus saw before plunging a dagger into Caesar's back was the expression on his mother's face. Expressions like this, whether on the faces of men or of women, are what map out the development of our history, rather than more complicated issues that we have been led to think about for years: the beginning and the end of everything, let me repeat myself, is the theatre.

This, this frown between Valle's eyebrows, is the last thing I remember with any clarity from this first meeting, that and the joyful hugging in the semidarkness and also the empty and premeditated sound of the Olivetti Lettera adding my name to the list of members of the Sincerity League.

Although at first sight the opposite might appear to be the case, Heliberto Sagredo is an extremely active person, with a busy schedule, at least between the hours of 18:00 and 21:00, which is when Valle (I'm not going to call her Thursday any more) and I are down to keep an eye on him. You might say that he lives in a constant state of transit. Round about six p.m. he heads out of the door, dragging a shopping trolley (sometimes a shopping basket) and heads to the Red Circle supermarket a couple of blocks from his house. Normally, probably for reasons of mobility, he tries not to walk on the pavements. When it is not raining, what he does is walk in the road, taking advantage of the fact that the traffic is coming from the other direction.

Within the limitations of his weight, which is more than one hundred and fifty kilos (I am a witness to this, having seen in the chemist's shop how the needle on the scale went down to this magnificent figure), Sagrado can consider himself an elegant and even dapper man. So if you have been thinking of him as shabby and smelly, a slob, then please, put your prejudices to one side. Lacoste polo shirts and black pleated trousers are the basis of his wardrobe, and in a recurring daydream I imagine him sliding his large open hand among the coat hangers and stroking the secret rainbow that hangs in his wardrobe. Valle, on the other hand, likes to think of him sitting in the bathroom, covered in foam, like a generous, smiling and damp Buddha. Whether divinity or guardian of the rainbow, Heliberto Sagredo is very popular in the Red Circle and the staff, at the checkout and stacking the shelves, treat him well. After paying for his purchases, he always leaves a set of keys at the till so that one of the staff (Sagredo does not have a preference in this matter) can take the trolley or basket of purchases up to his flat.

The rest of the afternoon Sagredo spends with the gang. I was going to leave the question of the gang here, but for those of you who are not *au fait* with the cultural heritage of Bilbao, it is an issue that needs a certain amount of explanation. Imagine a philosopher from Classical Greece, Aristotle or Socrates, either one would do, and imagine him walking along a cobbled street, with his pupils following close behind; all of them, master and pupils alike, with their hands behind their back; a scent of basil and oregano in the air; in the distance, where the horizon ends, twilight is falling on the columns of the Parthenon. Now change the décor; get rid of the Parthenon and replace it with smoking industrial chimneys; fill the horizon with buildings made from red brick, cranes and concrete skeletons of abandoned building projects; add streets, highways, cars, traffic lights, streetlamps and shops. And finally, change the protagonists: instead of a philosopher and ten or a dozen pupils, incorporate ten or twelve philosophers, a dozen men who all think they know everything about everything. And now send them marching from bar to bar. Well, that's the gang.

The barcrawl finishes at around nine p.m. At this time, our man, slightly tipsy, says farewell to the last survivors, unlocks his flat and heads up in the lift. Three minutes later, while Valle and I are looking for a place where we can say goodbye properly, a dense blue light starts to be visible from his balcony.

On 6 July, when all the members of our group are free from our scholarly obligations, we fire the starting-gun for the operation. That day, at ten past six in the afternoon (it might have been quarter past or even twenty past), as soon as Sagredo's belly appears past the glass door of his apartment block, I shout out my first 'fucking whale', crouched down on the ground between a Renault Cinco and a Supermirafiori. He seems to take the insult calmly: he adjusts the handle of the shopping trolley in his hand and barely shakes his recently washed head from side to side. Of course, although it is impossible to know exactly what he is thinking at this moment, he has received

88

a whole rosary of insults from other members of the League over the course of the day, and it is probably fair enough to think that by now the overdose of 'medicine' is starting to lose its effectiveness. His sluggishness could also be attributable to the excessive heat of the day, more than thirty-five degrees Centigrade, which has turned the air into jam, and the street into an abandoned field of burning hot car bonnets and asphalt trembling at its melting point: a sort of giant piece of chewing gum, which the cars have stuck to like bright and vulgar leftover food.

Valle is keeping watch underneath the balcony of a first-floor flat, about thirty metres further on. Fatty, you've got a dick like a peanut, I hear her say as I zigzag between the cars on the way to our meeting-point, a little square nearby with a chessboard pavement. About thirty seconds later my girlfriend arrives full tilt, with her hair mussed up and two large wheels of sweat under her arms.

'Oof,' she says and throws herself into my arms. 'I ran so much.'

That afternoon we carry out two further actions: Valle has suggested that we work together. The first takes place in the Red Circle and consists in a series of porcine grunts that we are able to utter with impunity, given the labyrinthine nature of the supermarket. The second is a chalk drawing on the glass door of the victim's apartment block, a *ligne clair* caricature with exaggerated roundnesses, labelled 'A Lard-arse Lives Here'. As soon as he sees it, Sagredo leaves his friends and devotes all his energy to rubbing away the picture and the letters and leaving only a foggy outline. Then, with his hands still covered in chalk, he drops his vast behind on the white-flecked grey marble step into his building. The advance guard of a stream of liquid starts to flow down his left cheek. Valle says it is sweat; I think it is tears. In any case, we are both too far away to be sure. What is certain is that the blue light takes a lot longer than normal to be seen on Sagredo's balcony.

It is hard for me to get to sleep that night, and when I finally manage, my sleep is a broken mockery, a choppy torment that rattles like a goods train. Every time I close my eyes, the strangest thoughts flow through my limp brain, inconsistent, like stitches in a long and twisted hemline. For some time, an hour, two hours, three hours (my periods of semi-wakefulness are, as I suppose is the case for everyone, impossible to measure and expand and contract according to rules I have no idea about whatsoever), I go over in my mind how the day must have been for the rest of the League: I can hear Monday and Tuesday murmuring in a lift after having slid a note under Sagredo's door; then I see them running among the morning crowd, holding each others' hand, Monday's head sticking up out of the multitude like a periscope, I can hear their lips smacking together in a kiss that seems more like a fight than a kiss. Then Wednesday meets Sagredo face to face, but instead of words, huge spit bubbles come out of his Mongol mouth, bubbles that are so huge that they have cars inside them, planes, whole buildings that fly through the air weightless with who knows what destination or design. Then, suddenly, Sagredo's head starts to get bigger and bigger, just like the bubbles, and our mouths (the mouths of all the members of the League) start to spin round it, spitting out all kinds of crude language: lardarse, greasy bastard, monster, gutbucket, porky, etcetera. This final part of the story must have occurred while I actually was asleep, because without any transition whatsoever, I find myself (this is how I note it down in my diary the next morning) thinking that the theatre has its limitations as well, just like life and that, without having to look further for examples, neither is very good at representing dreams.

The routine insults continue with the varied success of such behaviour until Friday afternoon, when Sagredo's children, the twins Estela and Mar, ring the bell of what until very recently was their home because they want to spend the weekend with their father. He, after his initial incredulity and reluctance, and a long conversation over the intercom, lets them in with few complaints. It is about as hot as it has been for the past few days and on the pavement across the road, Valle and myself, wanting shade more than concealment, have seen the whole thing from the glass-fronted crucible of a newspaper kiosk. This was where we spent the afternoon waiting for Sagredo's afternoon departure from his house, and we had been there until we heard a sudden noise of brakes and seen the two girls getting down from a Simca. They are identical. For all that you might try to find a difference between them you never lose the sensation, a little magical and quite a lot sinister, that what you are looking at is a single girl recently divided in two, like one of those single-celled organisms (amoebas, paramecia, bacteria and so on) who reproduce by splitting themselves into two equal halves.

That afternoon, at Valle's urgent request, the League reconvenes urgently to think about this new situation. In brief, the possible options are two: to call a halt, for humanitarian reasons, to the attacks on Sagredo while his children are with him, or else to intensify our attack in the hope that, with his *amour-propre* under severe attack, Sagredo will turn his life around in a radical fashion and take the necessary steps to turn himself into a new man. Taking the decision keeps us locked in the office until nearly midnight. Over three long hours the walls, poorly lit by the pair of candles, fill up with shadows that stretch and gesture. Monday and Tuesday, with a vehemence that seems to contain both conviction and fanaticism, especially the latter, insist from the start that we should not stop our assaults, and like magical swords sunk into granite rocks, they remain immoveable throughout the whole evening. Valle and I are in favour of stopping the mission until Estela and Mar are back with their mother. We are sure that the father's being humiliated in the presence of his daughters will pass similar sensations on to them, and that whatever the feelings that our 'target' has for us (hatred, anger, disdain, even a sunken and invisible desire for revenge), will end up affecting the children. At a deadlock in this way (Monday and Tuesday in favour of continuing, Valle and myself keen to pause), the decision has to be submitted to Wednesday, whose ability to pass judgement is more than anything else like a Mexican desert: scorched earth, dust, the occasional cactus. Wednesday puts his right hand round his chin, walks two or three times across the room, closes his Mongol eyes and after puffing out and deflating his round cheeks in an inimitable series of sighs, stammers: We'll wait. Monday writes the result of the vote with the old Olivetti and we leave the office in silence and in single file. The night has scarcely got any cooler and is dense and sticky. On the horizon, among the streets and the cars, a crescent moon makes the roofs shine a coppery colour.

On Monday, early in the morning, while we are all having breakfast, coffee and croissants, in a café near to Sagredo's building, Estela and Mar get back into the back seat of the Simca. The car is being driven by the children's mother, who does not even stop the car to shake her husband's extended, empty hand. Sagredo stands at the edge of the street with a cigarette in his mouth, watching the chestnut hair of his daughters disappearing from view until they are lost in the urban sprawl. Then, after a while, he stubs out his cigarette on the sole of his deck shoe and starts walking down the street, without aim or purpose, like a huge wounded animal. We agree that Monday and Tuesday will follow him while the rest of us stay in the café. Sagredo carries on down the street with his vague steps. Above his head, coming from the northeast, a huge clump of black clouds approaches across the blue of the sky. Sagredo looks up, and, after a few seconds of doubt or perhaps confusion, turns and retraces his steps with large strides. The pursued becomes the pursuer, or at least that's what Monday must think, as he starts running without telling Tuesday about the danger they're in. With hardly any time to react, Tuesday is in the path of Sagredo as he approaches, like a single skittle at the mercy of a ball that grows larger and larger as it approaches. There is no time for her to start running, that's for sure, so she decides to do nothing, to stand stock-still on the pavement. When Sagredo reaches her, Tuesday (she will never know what gave her such an extravagant idea) says hello, and Sagredo says hello back to her, friendly but a little disheartened. A moment later, Sagredo goes through his doorway; Tuesday, at a safe distance, goes back to the café as some heavy drops start to wet the streets. I remember that as she tells us her story among the empty cups and sticky croissant-stained plates, Tuesday is paying more attention to the rain falling down the café windows than to us and to her own story.

Over the next few days we increase the pressure on Sagredo, and even when he's at home (eating or sitting down and watching the telly, to name but two of his favourite activities) we ring his bell to reel off a list of unpleasant insults, more or less offensive depending on the will of the insulter: Monday and Tuesday prefer the classics: lardarse, sausage gut above all; Valle, more refined but much more cruel, prefers subtlety along the lines of 'when you piss you can't see your dick', or 'calling Sagredo, overweight and out', or 'where did you leave the other two little pigs?'; Wednesday's mouth only expels naïve variations on a theme: fatso, fatty, all derivatives of 'fat' that because of his stammer stick to his mouth like it was a rubber slide; as for me I try to say the first thing that comes into my head, which is nothing, or else I repeat like a parrot something that someone else has already said. If, in the face of this onslaught of doorbelling, Sagredo refuses to pick up the intercom, then we stick a sunflower seed round the bell, so that it rings and doesn't stop ringing. Then, a few minutes later, swearing fit to turn the air purple, Sagredo comes down in shorts and slippers to take the seed out and we, from the other side of the street, take this opportunity to attack him until we are all tired out: fatso, black pudding, lardarse, creampuff and other pleasant words. This daily ritual, except when Sagredo calls the police or when the windows fill with curious onlookers, can be extended for an hour or more from the first ring on the bell until the final insults in the street.

When we know in advance where Sagredo is going, then we plan activities, a verbal simulacrum of a skirmish in a war. We stand along the route he will take in strategic spaces (crossroads, traffic lights and stairways, in general) and insult him with impunity, but by now, with his sense of self-worth well and truly exploded, Sagredo scarcely puts up any resistance, and even less seems to be holding anything back in order to fight back at any point.

It would be possible for the cinema to record these sequences exactly, giving it a skilful sheen. Sagredo would walk along, dragging his shopping basket behind him in the July sun. Sweat would fall in sheets down his forehead and would also appear in its more subtle guises, sketching dark circles under his armpits and a huge oval in the small of his back. Suddenly, a series of insults would explode in the oppressive summer air, and Sagredo's face would appear in extreme close-up in the screen: stretched out, in a rictus of extreme exhaustion, close to despair and abandoned hope. Then the camera, from

Sagredo's point of view, would lift up to film a general shot of the sky: a dark blue duvet fillet with ashy clouds. In the theatre, we would only have a static, matte stage, existential, which would go on for longer than necessary and make more than one audience member yawn.

On a day when we had agreed to engage in intensive activity, the telephone rings in my house very early, it must be only just past eight. My parents have gone out to work and I have no intention of picking it up, but it keeps on ringing and finally I get up and answer it grumpily. It's Tuesday: he's dead, she says. Who? I ask. Sagredo, she says, who else would it be. He threw himself off his balcony. I say nothing for a moment than hang up. Then I call Valle and tell her what has happened, and we go to the scene half an hour later. The damage caused by Sagredo's fall is noticeable on the pavement, and the police are cordoning off the area. A few operatives have wrapped Sagredo's balcony in a metallic cage.

That morning we decide unanimously to dissolve the League and not to see each other for a long time. If we meet anywhere, whether or not there are witnesses, we are to pretend that we do not know each other. The next day I find out in the newspaper that Sagredo's balcony gave way under his weight and that what we thought was a suicide was in fact an accident. I call Valle, but she does not want to speak to me. She does not want to speak to me on any of the dozens of times that I call in the days and weeks that follow. When I meet Wednesday by accident at the beginning of September, I find out that Valle has gone to Salamanca to study Psychology. Every year since then, on the day of what would have been our anniversary, I go to the cemetery and put a bouquet of carnations on Heliberto Sagredo's grave. Once I even run into his daughters, who were tidying up the headstone, but I don't say anything to them. I leave the bouquet on another tomb that time. Both of them are fat, weighty, and when they walk quickly, the ground in the cemetery, as if it were a weak theatrical stage, threatens to give way under their feet.

5. [Triangle]

One Million Pounds

I TELL ÞÓRA THAT I'M GOING TO THE PET SHOP FOR BIRDSEED, knowing that I will never come back. I have spent years fighting against the idea that it's going to have to happen one day; but one morning, after a nightmare, almost without wanting to, my right hand reaches out for a biro and the calendar on the bedside table and my left hand strikes off the first of September in the darkness. It is very difficult to live with the knowledge that a few hours away by plane, in a hole near Chorleywood (Hertfordshire), a million pounds is buried and only two people know exactly where; and the other one is in prison.

It was a simple and clean job, I'll tell no lies. We intercepted the armoured truck at the agreed time, we neutralised the agents without killing them and we blew the safe with a chunk of plastic explosive. Then we left the guards tied up and gagged in a nearby hunters' cabin, took off our balaclavas, swapped the Austin for another car, an old black MG 1100, and looked for a suitable spot to bury the dough. It was getting dark when the last few shovelfuls of clayey earth covered the hole we had marked with a cross on the map (each of us had his own map, with his own cross on it, as well as a fake passport in case things got sticky). Harry opened the boot and we threw the shovels in. He lost no time in getting into the car and turning on the lights and the engine. Ed and I got in the back. The gloves were too small for me and I wanted to take them off, but Harry must have seen me in the rearview mirror. Are you nuts, Ethan, he shouted, at least wait until all this shit's over with. Ed, who had taken off his right glove, put it back on without complaint. For about half an hour we drove along a minor road past green hills and summer homes. The night had closed in, was cold, and the wheels of the MG were covered in dust and pebbles kept on being thrown up against the headlights and the bonnet. When we were just about to leave the road, turn onto an A-road, the front right headlamp went out. Harry stopped on the verge and ducked out of the car. It's blown, he swore, we've got to change it. There weren't any spare bulbs in the glove compartment or the boot, but we thought we should go to the closest petrol station, ten miles away, and get some. The prisons are filled with people who didn't take care, who got pulled over by the police for a broken headlight, I'm not telling you anything you don't know already. Harry turned the engine on again and we turned towards the petrol station, but coming off a curve, in a black and woody place, we found a Morris stopped across the middle of the road, which made him slam the brakes on. Ed and I nearly left our teeth in the seats in front of us. A little shaken up, we got carefully out of the car and went to see what was up. The Morris was empty, but the motor was still running, even if the lights were off, and the radio was playing 'My Generation' by The Who. Harry, scratching one of his immense sideburns, said that he didn't like the look of this, but he got behind the wheel to see if he could get the car off the road. Meanwhile, Ed and I, pistols in hand, stood at the back of the car in case it became necessary to push. The Morris hadn't moved an inch when a bullet hit Harry in the temple. He was thrown back against his seat. The next shots hit the body of the car and Ed's right calf: he twisted with pain and shuffled under the car, covering me while I looked for a better spot to fire from by the wing of the car. It was clear that, taking advantage of the darkness and the foliage, one or maybe two men were firing at us from the right edge of the wood. I fired in that direction, and after the third or fourth shot I heard a grown, and then a hollow sound that could just be heard above the noise of The Who and their guitars. The next thing I remember is hearing the distant sound of police sirens: they had obviously been alerted by the petrol station after the shots were fired; I also remember Ed, his head against a tyre, chewing his map and telling me to take Harry's and get out of there as quickly as I could.

I took the map from Harry's jacket and a torch from the Morris's glove compartment, turned off the radio and headed into the wood. I almost trod on the legs of the fucker who had been shooting at us. He was just a kid. His hair was long and he was wearing combat-print jeans, and there was a hole in his chest. That's all I can say about him, I only saw him for a few seconds. The sirens were still in the distance, but it would have been a risk to keep the torch lit for any longer. I spent the next hour or so running through weeds and past thin-trunked trees, and then, when my running turned into a pathetic trot, I climbed over several hedges that ran parallel to the main road into Essex. I couldn't see that I was being followed: no whistles, no barking dogs, no helicopters, but a police car could be waiting for me just when I least expected it. And this, along with the exhaustion made me feel as if I had a mad hamster running around in my arse. My plan, if you can call it such, was to get to Harwich and once there, with the false passport, to head as far as I could from England. But I still had a lot of miles to go to get there, and I did not really want to travel by foot. So I put my pistol down the back of my trousers, took off the damn gloves and stood by the edge of the road, hitchhiking. Thanks to two chunky farmers, I managed to travel the first few miles in a trailer pulled by a tractor, among bundles of straw and bags of seeds. Then, when I stuck my hand out again, I got a taciturn lorry driver who offered to take me to Harwich docks itself, on the Stour and Orwell estuary. I stayed in the docks for a while, hitting the beers and flirting with women and singing songs as if I were a sailor or just one more stevedore with his hands covered in coaldust. I know that this was quite foolish and I exposed myself unnecessarily, but the first boat, a Copenhagen steamer, didn't leave until seven, and the only other options open to me were to try to sleep for a while on one of the stone benches on the dock, or else to walk down to the breakwater and watch the ships coming and going, both of which seemed to me to be much more suspicious activities than hanging around in pars with whores and old sea dogs.

Before boarding, while I took the first few sips of burning hot coffee at the metal bar of a café, I heard on the radio that two men had been killed and a third had been wounded in a shootout in Hertfordshire. Apparently, the announcer said, it had been a confrontation between criminals and members of the IRA. They didn't say anything about me or about the job. I suppose that it was better for the bank and its insurer to keep quiet about it, but it took me a while, several years, to come to that conclusion. All that occurred to me then was that Ed must have sung like a canary and that the fuzz were trying to set a trap for me. My thoughts about the kid were twofold: either he had got the wrong car or else he was just an idiot with no connection to the IRA, and the police, whether for their own interests or else simply by accident, had confused him with a terrorist. These thoughts kept me busy for a good part of the crossing and even, when my pistol, wrapped in Harry's map, slipped into the Atlantic, made me doubt that I was doing the right thing.

I got a job on an oil platform in the North Sea a few days after reaching Copenhagen. The company needed an English native to fill in paperwork and deal with clients, and in spite of my lack of references I must have seemed perfect for them. My little floating Babel contained about two hundred people, including welders, electricians, painters, waiters, laundrymen, cooks, engineers, submariners, labourers, administrators etcetera. We worked in forty-five day shifts (a working day of ten hours followed by fourteen hours of rest) followed by fifteen days off. When it was a worker's turn to rest, someone else took his place. Life was tedious, a heavy and burdensome chain of work, life and breaking waves, but the pay, in US dollars, was excellent. I decided to invest part of my first pay check in getting to know Iceland. And that was how I met Þóra.

When I set foot back in London I realise that the centre of the City has suffered only light changes since my departure: many more tourists in Trafalgar Square, new benches in Hyde Park from which to throw pieces of bread to the ducks, swans and geese in the Serpentine, streets closed to traffic in the West End... However, it's enough for me to see night falling over an open Tower Bridge, with the white light of the lamps along the Thames, for me to feel a quiver along my upper lip and to understand that the time I spent out of England, in the North Sea and in Reykjavík, with Þóra, was borrowed time, which did not belong to me and to which I did not belong. I loved Þóra in my fashion, with all ifs and buts firmly in place, and I still feel a certain affection for her, but Saebraut and its bright coloured houses, and Reykjavík as well, were just another cage for me whose only difference from the others, Þóra's birdcages, was that the bars were not made of wires, but were instead bars of the mind. I think Þóra must have been aware of my refusal to engage fully with her world, of my silent estrangement from it; and perhaps her obsession with taking photographs of me in tedious daily situations, non-transcendent environments, hitting a nail with a hammer or stirring a saucepan, and her desire for me to do the same with her, were the result of an impulse to rescue occasional intimate moments, moments which she could consider blessed, or even happy.

I spend the night of my return in a hotel in Leicester Square, close to the row and hubbub of Piccadilly Circus. In the morning, I rent an ivory-coloured Dodge 1500 and buy a bright shiny shovel and one hundred and seventy four feet of rope in a shop on Beak Street. The owner of the shop, a chubby, jocular type, makes no objection when I ask him to make me a mark at one hundred and five feet. With the windows down, I drive slowly into Hertfordshire. I enjoy every light on the horizon, every wheat field and every planted space that stands by the motorway behind the hawthorn hedges. Five kilometres from Chorleywood, once I pass the petrol station and the turnoff where all this mess started, I stop on the verge to check the map once more. I am sure that I need to take the first turn off to the left, but the next steps, especially the path I need to follow to get me to the hole, are not sufficiently clear in my memory.

The evening before, with the pillow twisted under my head, I have looked in detail at the piece of paper (or I thought that was what I was doing), but now it's as if my eyes had passed over it without understanding it at all; and my fingers, instead of running over the contours, had just felt the rough and harsh texture of the map. For the last few years the map has stayed hidden in a hermetically sealed jar in the cistern in our bathroom, as if it were a message from a man shipwrecked in the middle of a desert, hoping that his words would one day make it to the sea. I had only taken it out of there on five or six previous occasions, just for the simple greed of holding it in my hands again, usually after having had an argument with Þóra, and never opening the top. Now, out of the cistern, out of its jar, I do not enjoy looking at it so much; in fact, I sometimes doubt if I should have it at all, and sometimes I am even tempted by the crazy idea that somehow or other I have swapped places with the map, and that it is now me inside the jar.

The money is buried to the northeast of a field, one hundred and seventy four feet (one hundred and five straight forwards and sixty nine to the right) away from a electricity pole by the side of a dusty road, but as soon as I park the car and look up, I can see that although the post is still there it will be useless to unwind the rope. In the direction that I should travel there is now a house, a white house with a steepled roof and a garden and a pergola, with rose bushes and statues of dolphins heaving themselves over a green fence. I am almost sure that the hundred and five feet would take me into the grounds of the building, either into the garden or into one of the rooms of the house: the living room, the pantry, the kitchen or even the bathroom (and here I start to worry a lot about the possibility that a million pounds, just like the map that led to it, might end up in a bathroom, even underground). But if I want to get the money back, and I am prepared to do anything to get it back, then there is no option open to me other than to cross the fence and ring the bell with my best smile on my face. If there is a chance in a thousand of getting the dough, I want to keep going until I find it.

The gate in the fence is half open. I push it gently, cross the threshold and take a few steps forward. When I am alongside a yellow dolphin, I hear a noise, a cooing sound, and stop. A lilt girl with a rag doll in her arms comes out from behind the dolphin. She is very tall for her age, about six or seven, and her large eyes, which are a dull brown and a little bulgy, remind me of those of a chameleon.

'Hello.'

'Shhh, keep your voice down, sir. Coro, my doll, has just got off to sleep, but I need to keep an eye on her all the time. She walks in her sleep, and if I don't keep an eye on her, she could have an accident.'

'Don't worry, I'll be quiet. Can you tell your mother I'd like to talk with her?'

'Alright, but stay here and don't whistle or anything; Coro could wake up.'

'Don't worry, I'll stay here just as quietly and as peacefully as those dolphins. And now, be a good girl and go and tell your mother.'

The girl climbs the four stone steps that lead up to the house very slowly, and taking great care that the door doesn't slam behind her, she goes indoors. White curtains twitch for a moment behind a window, and half a minute later the door opens again. The girl, without the doll this time, appears clutching her mother's hand. Her mother clicks her tongue.

'Luana told me that you want to speak with me,' she says with a South American accent, which could be from Argentina, or Uruguay, or even Chile. 'What can I do for you?'

'I saw the dolphins from the road.'

'And you like them?'

'Yes, and I think they'd look good in my garden, but I don't know where I could buy some like them. That's why I took the liberty of coming in, to see them from close up and to talk with the owner. Then I met your daughter. Well, it was really her who met me.'

'They are made out of terracotta. I sculpt them and fire them and paint them myself. So, if you really want to order some, then you have come to the right place. Come on, come in, don't stand out here like a statue. We'll be able to talk business better over a cup of coffee. My name is Mirta Varsavsky and this beanpole is my daughter Luana.'

The girl starts pulling again and again at her mother's arm, until she finally gives in and bends down to hear what her daughter wants to whisper in her ear.

'Alright, darling. Mister...'

'Darius Horrocks,' I say.

'Mister Horrocks and I will speak very quietly so as not to wake Coro.'

Mirta Varsavsky's living room is like a charity bazaar. There is a large gilded gramophone in the middle of the room, with three piles of records to its left. Luana's toys are piled up against one of the walls in a heap: a gallery of horrors that includes, amongst other relics, a bunch of separate meccano pieces, storybooks with the covers and most of the pages torn out, headless teddy bears and dolls that are blind, bald or crippled or else all three at the same time. On the three remaining walls are a red corner sofa, which is currently serving as Coro's improvised bed, and a black leather chaise longue, where Mirta invites me to sit while she retires to the kitchen to make coffee. Luana, meanwhile, removes a plastic cradle from the volcanic crater that is her heap of toys, settles Coro in it on the red sofa, and blankets her with a napkin. The remaining time she spends walking round the sofa on tiptoe, pulling her ears and showing me her tongue, much less chameleon-like than her eyes, until she hears a squeaking sound and heads back to the sofa to watch over Coro's sleep. Mirta comes into the room pushing a trolley that contains an Italian coffee-maker, a jug of milk, two cups, two spoons, a sugar bowl and a tray of cakes made from quince jelly and coconut. She parks the trolley at the foot of the chaise longue, sits down next to me, and pours coffee for us both.

It takes little more than a quarter of an hour to close the deal for the dolphins. We agree that Mirta will make me six: two red, two white, and two blue. I prefer green to blue, but she insists that the green dolphins get lost among the foliage, so I let her decide. We do not discuss the price. I offer her five hundred pounds per dolphin and see from her face that this price must be more than welcome to her.

The rest of the conversation is on personal matters, as must normally happen when people from very different backgrounds end up talking to each other, especially when they need to mutter through their teeth so as not to wake a doll. Mirta, without my asking her, gets me up to speed with all the reversals of fortune and chance happenings that have led her from the salt-water lagoon at Mar Chiquita (in Cordoba, Argentina), an idyllic spot of high and low coastlines, wetlands, beaches, sunny days and cool breezy evenings, all the way to what I see as the sober and self-contained county of Hertfordshire, and what she sees as the boring, grey and spiritless county of Hertfordshire.

Luana has been the centre of the last few years in Mirta's life as well as the driving force behind all these changes. Mirta Varsavsky comes from a wealthy family (owners of a hotel complex on the banks of the Ansenuza Sea), protective by nature; but when Mirta gets pregnant in the last year of her Fine Arts degree and opts to be a single mother, protection transforms itself into harassment. Helped by their financial clout, in the face of Mirta's refusal to tell them the name of her daughter's father, the family—the mother in particular—insist on trying to find another father for the little mite while it is still growing inside its mother's belly. For five or six unbearable months, Mirta is forced to spend time with upstarts of all kinds, guys with dopey smiles and suits that smell of mothballs who take their opportunity to bend an ear to Mirta's stomach and listen to the foetus, although most of them hear nothing but a celestial clinking as of golden coins. Mirta trusts that when she gives birth her parents' pressure on her to get married will lessen a little, but quite the contrary, they get even more demanding. And so, fed up with so many asphyxiating displays of hypocrisy, when Luana reaches her first birthday, Mirta takes her from her cradle at midnight and the two of them, with only a single suitcase and a wash kit for the journey, take a taxi to Antonio Taravella airport, fly to Ezeiza international airport in Buenos Aires, and take the first available flight to London.

The first weeks they stay in an apartment belonging to Luci, a friend from university who has begun work as a restorer in the National Gallery. Luci recommends Mirta for a job in the Gallery cloakroom and, with her first paycheck, Mirta rents a room for herself and Luana in the East End and employs a Bengali woman to look after the child while she is at work. Opposite the flat, at the bottom of the street, is a shop that sells handicrafts. At night, when Luana wakes up crying, Mirta picks her up and takes her to the window, where her daughter calms down gazing at the red neon light of the shop and its window filled with statues, candlesticks and masks. The window, and by extension the shop, are the only distractions in a room in which the loo is separated from the tiny gas stove by only a couple of feet.

One afternoon, coming back from the museum, Mirta decides to go into the shop. She has had a horrible day, dealing with an endless queue of visitors, and the palms of her hands are scraped from hanging and unhanging so many coats. Mirta goes to speak to the owner, an old woman who, sitting on a high stool, is drawing languidly on a pipe, and says, without beating around the bush, that she is a sculptor and that, if she can sell some of her work in the shop, then she will let the owner keep half the profits. The old woman, Betty Fraser, accepts the offer, and a week later Mirta and Luci go into the shop with a pink dolphin on their shoulders, so large it barely fits through the door. It is a realistic sculpture, apart from its impossible colour: it has a very long muzzle, an aerodynamic body shaped like a spindle, and little fins which Mirta has twisted into an attractive display of acrobatic endeavour. A month later, the waiting list has more than twenty people on it.

Mirta leaves her job and takes the necessary steps, using Betty Fraser's contacts, for the business to carry on growing. Then there's a little flat in Greenwich, a bungalow in Barnet, and finally the purchase of a piece of land in Herefordshire, where Mirta builds her house on top of my million pounds.

Over these years, from the first day she arrives in London, she keeps her parents informed of her movements, but refuses any economic help from them. As time goes by, the tyranny of the paterfamilias relaxes slightly, and Mirta makes a few concessions: Luana spends her summer holidays with her grandparents, and they make an effort to see each other every other Christmas.

Told in this way, as a simple series of events, this might seem like a straightforward narrative, maybe even too straightforward, too linear, but Mirta adds a number of extra points, sidetracks, which I can't repeat here, not because I disapprove of them or because I find them unattractive, but because as she unfolds to me her recent life I feel the need to build my own one up in the void; I don't want her to get curious and then, suspicious. Luckily enough, during this first meeting I barely need to speak, and when Luana says with a wide smile that Coro has just woken up, I take a glance at my watch, and using an unavoidable appointment as an excuse, I take a note of Mirta's phone number on one piece of paper, leave the name of my hotel on another, and leave the living room.

Even so, Mirta Varsavsky's story keeps running through my mind, even as the house, the dolphins and the green fence disappear from the rear-view mirror. The fact that Mirta chose London, city of choice for thousands of women in search of an abortion, as the site for her to begin her new life with Luana, seems a stroke of antideterminism. Moreover, in its initial episodes, Mirta's story has a disconcerting number of parallels with my life over the last few years: both of us fled a long way, from family pressures in her case and from the threat of prison in mine; both of us were forced to inhabit claustrophobic environments, she in a single room, me in an oil-rig; and to a certain extent, she more than me, we found our various refuges in Luana and dolphins or Þóra and birds. You could say that there are only one hundred and seventy four feet separating us.

I spend the next few days on tenterhooks. I left Þóra without even leaving her a quick goodbye note, and the most likely situation is that she is now on the edge of a nervous breakdown, living on tranquilisers and hoping for the phone to ring, with half the Reykjavík police force searching for my body in alleyways, beaches and geysers. If it had been any other woman, just some woman, from the slums of Mogadishu or the south of Patagonia, the cards would have been on the table from the beginning, but I can't take risks with Þóra. If she had heard anything about me, then either she would have fallen back in her chair and done nothing, or she would have sold the house, and left the birds with a neighbour and gone on to plan a thorough and rigorous revenge. The best for me, for all that my silence makes me feel pitiless and mean, is to let time slowly unstitch me from her head. Also, my plans for the money and for Mirta are uncertain and confused. I can't let myself call her all the time, but there's no point in my waiting for the phone to ring either. Either option is bad for my aim, which is to win her confidence. I spend this time of uncertainty and fear taking long walks round the city and looking up back issues of *The Guardian* in the local lending library. This is how I find out that in the months following my flight there was no news at all about the job, and that Ed died of pneumonia in Pentonville. Ed was agnostic and liked fishing, so although my initial impulse is to leave a bouquet of white chrysanthemums on his tombstone, the most likely thing is that his ashes have been scattered at one of his favourite spots on the East Coast. As for Harry, they buried him in Putney Vale, in east London, and on one rainy morning, the kind he liked so much, on a whim I leave a pair of leather gloves on his gravestone. They are not the ones I wore for the job, they're not even the same colour or size, mine were black and these are brown and much bigger, but I'm sure that if he could see them, Harry would run a hand through his left sideburn and thank me for thinking of him.

Mirta does not reappear in my life the next week. Nor the week after that. Almost three weeks have gone by and the only thing I have managed is to feel more regret about Þóra and about the half dozen clay cetaceans which still have no fixed delivery date, and which I have no idea of where they will go. To plan the way in which the next few stages of the plan will develop is going to require a great deal of foresight on my part, but my terrace, rather than blooming with plant life, is much more like the shadowy vegetation of Putney Vale, with its stony and labyrinthine architecture and sparse vegetation punctuated every now and then with cypresses. If I really want to get away with my million pounds (always assuming that they are not being thrown around in some Mallorcan bay by the engineer and the construction workers who built Mirta's house), then a conventional map is not going to be enough, however secret and non-transferable it might be; I need another kind of map, with all possibilities plotted out on it, all the inevitable dilemmas: what to do or what not to do, how to do it or how not to do it; above all, when to act.

On the morning of Friday, 21 September, I rent a Land Rover, put the spade and the rope inside, and drive to Mirta's house. The day is windy and glum, dark clouds scudding overhead. I park on the right-hand edge of the road and, with the ignition turned off, stay in the driver's seat and for the hundredth time look at the map spread over the steering wheel. A cloud of saffron-coloured dust is blown over the hood, and a good part of the floating particles end up on the windscreen, which becomes an archipelago of dirt. I try to look at the map again. If the map is correct—and I can find no absolutely convincing arguments why this should be so—then the hundred and seventy-four paces (one hundred and five forwards and sixty-nine to the right) must start just at the edge of the road, next to this cable-bearing post that Harry marked as the point of reference on the map. If the post had gone by the time we came back, which is not the case, as I noticed the first time I was here, the reserve indicator was a milepost showing the distances to Chorleywood and other nearby places, marked on the back of the map. The post is still in place, as I have already said, but if it had not been, then the signpost would have been an equally valid referent. In any case without knowing if there is anyone at home, there's no point in stretching out the rope until I reach the mark at the hundred and five foot point, and even less point in then heading right into the house, under the fence. As an alternative, instead of using the rope, I could count out the distance in paces: forty forwards and twenty-six to the right, which was how Harry did it as well on the afternoon of the job, as a final security measure: the numbers are written, sinuously, sick and so twisted they look like greyhounds on the back of the map as well. Of course Harry's paces aren't the same as mine, or the same as 'average' paces. And the ones he took back then and the ones I am going to take now are not the same. But this could give me an idea of the approximate spot where the money is buried, and if Mirta is at home, then the intention behind taking a few paces is probably more easy to conceal than a hundred and fifty foot rope.

The first part of the task, forty paces, takes me close to the fence, and ends up five paces past the metal gate. I take this in my stride, walk back to the gate and ring the doorbell, ready to take the next twenty-six paces somehow or other. Mirta appears immediately at an upstairs window. Her hair is tied back in a tight ponytail, like Þóra used to wear hers, and her lower lip twists a little when she sees me; but after this initial shock, and when I shout up to her that I came across here by chance and wanted to know how my dolphins were getting along, I think she feels flattered.

'Come in and wait for me, Darius,' she chivvies me. 'The dolphins are behind the house and are scarcely floating yet, but I'll show them to you anyway. Give me five minutes,' she says and steps back from the window and closes it quickly, so quickly that I don't have time to thank her.

I walk through the gate and start my count. It's not a countdown, but a countup, but when I put my right foot forwards, I feel a shiver down my spine, a bubbling sensation of emptiness, as if I were an astronaut whose body hung suspended in the darkness of space, a cushioned body bobbing in the most worrying, weightless and slow-moving of wakes. I feel the ground soft beneath the soles of my shoes. Yesterday there were several downpours and between nine and five past nine the centre of London went dark, lit only by the electric storm that played on the horizon. The stormclouds, in fact, are still in the sky. They are still there, doubled up as if in pain, waiting perhaps for the wind to drop and give them a chance to expand and release their load. For the first ten paces I feel moderate optimism as far as the location of the million pounds is concerned and, Mirta not having come down yet, and knowing that she will take a while, I take the five paces to the left that I still need to complete, having needed to step back to get to the gate previously, and I find myself next to the yellow dolphin from behind which Luana and Coro, her sleepwalking doll, had appeared the first time I came here. I still have sixteen paces to take and several dolphins of various colours to leave behind me, but everything points to the idea that the distance between me and the house is more than these sixteen paces, and this, in principal, allows me to draw two tentative conclusions: the chances that the money is outside the house are high, and if it is at any distance from the foundations of the house, then it is also likely that the builders did not come across it. However, I take the next steps filled with fatalistic thoughts. My head is filled with the image of a basset hound, its dripping tongue flopping out of its mouth as it scrabbles in the earth that covers my money with its paws. Mirta herself, dressed in dungarees, kneeling down and engaged in the most lucrative piece of digging in the history of gardening. I also think that it's possible, if she uses the clay from her garden to make the dolphins, the money might have been accidentally baked inside one of them, ruined at more than two thousand degrees Farenheit. Then, as I get closer to the end and am concentrating harder so as not to lose count, my worries take another turn. Now I'm only interested in the margin of error that each pace might contain: are they shorter than Harry's? Perhaps a shade longer? In any case, what might my margin of error be? Five, ten, twenty paces. Have I gone past the money or is it still a long way ahead of me, under the house, with all the difficulties and problems that that will cause me? I am a wreck before I take the last step, smoothing my moustache, when I hear Mirta calling my name (Darius, my false name, my real name is Ethan): it comes out (because of the Argentine accent, I suppose) much more softly from between her lips than it did from between Þóra's, almost as if it were cushioned.

'Darius, what are you doing here?' she says from the top of the steps up to her house, holding her skirt with her thighs so that the wind doesn't blow it up. 'I told you the dolphins were round the back.'

'Yes, yes, I heard you,' I say, 'but I was just wondering if this paint was waterproof.' I point at the wall with my chin. 'It really rains, here doesn't it?'

Mirta smiles and her eyes sparkle naughtily. They are not as large as Luana's eyes and far less bulbous.

'Yes, that's right,' she says. 'And now, Darius, if you wouldn't mind, let's go and have a look at those dolphins before they fly away.'

The dolphins still have their first coat of muddy clay on, and are under a lean-to, waiting to be baked in a large muffle furnace alongside, a closed chamber lined with heat-resistant material. Mirta explains to me that she has thought of the commission as a little school (some of them seem to hang above the water, others seem to be rhythmically diving beneath the waves) and in order to reinforce the impression of the group, the idea is that they will all be put swimming in my garden in the same direction, following the same current. Then without giving me any further explanations, she grasps my forearm and says:

'You're hiding something from me. You can tell me the truth or you can lie, but the first option will make things much easier.'

'I don't have a clue what you're talking about. Let go of me,' I say. 'I've got to go.'

I take Mirta's hand off me, turn my back on her and head off into the wind, taking large paces. I am about to turn the corner of the house, prepared to settle the matter by any means necessary, when I hear her shouting:

'I've been watching you through the curtains, Darius Horrocks, and no one walks like that unless they're counting their paces.'

I come back quickly. Mirta is still where I left her, impassive underneath the lean-to. The wind is wheezing asthmatically and makes her skirt flap violently.

'I could finish you off right now,' I say. I don't intend to kill her, not in the least, but at the moment I don't think of anything better to say. I've gone crazy, there's no other explanation, and after this it will be very difficult for me to carry out my plans.

'Yes, you could, but you're not going to because you're not a killer,' she states bluntly. 'If you were, I'd be dead already.'

'What do you want?'

'Half,' she blurts out.

'Half of what?'

'Don't play the innocent with me, Darius.' The slackness with which she says my name really stings. I would hit her now, and gladly. 'You know what I'm talking about, all too well,' she adds.

'And if you're so sure about it, why don't you take it yourself?' I think that if I can get her into a corner (verbally, that is), then I'll be able to take her down, but that's a little like trying to get a raging river through the mouth of a carafe.

'I don't know where it is exactly,' she says. 'And if I did it alone, I'm sure you wouldn't hang around with your arms folded. I have a daughter to look after and the last thing I want are more problems.'

The allusion to Luana makes me look at the business from a different point of view. I realise that the fear of losing her daughter will close Mirta's mouth for ever and that this has just made her into my best possible ally. With Luana between us, Mirta wouldn't risk trying to cheat me. The girl is my insurance policy, and half a million pounds sterling is still a pretty good haul.

'Is there anyone else at home?' I ask.

Mirta takes two or three paces backwards, groping for the support the kiln can give her. Or maybe she's just trying to gain a second or two as she thinks up a suitable answer. My question must seem like a trap for her: one that can close as many doors as it opens.

'No, Luana's at school,' she says finally. 'The bus won't bring her back until after midday.'

'In that case we'll do it now.' When she hears this, Mirta jerks involuntarily. 'Listen to me. I want you to get into my car and keep your eyes open. If you see anything odd or if anyone stops close by, then sound the horn. Once. If it's the police, do it twice. You get it? I'll take care of the rest; you just do your bit.'

'OK,' she says and walks away.

A gust of wind reveals her thighs. They are pale and thin. She could have held the skirt down, but she lets the wind lift it and lower it. I give those disappearing legs a good look. Then I hurry over to her.

'Wait.' I tap Mirta's back gently. 'I'll come to the car with you. I need rope and a spade.'

The wind suddenly drops, and in the stillness a thin sidelong rain begins to fall. The first drops are as small as the head of a pin, you can see them on our shoes and they appear like dew on the rosebushes, the dolphins and the grass. A loose flock of noisy birds flies across our path heading south. Then the sky darkens and Mirta opens the gate as quickly as she can and runs across to the car. I follow close behind. In a few seconds we are seated in the front seat of the Land Rover (she's in the driver's seat, I'm in the passenger's seat), looking at the rain falling on the windows and the windscreen. I take a moment to realise that Mirta's eyes are filled with tears.

'What is it?' I ask.

'It's Luana,' she babbles. 'If anything happened to me, I don't know what would become of her.'

'Don't worry, nothing is going to happen to you or your daughter. The money has been there for a long time, and up until today the only person who has worried about it has been me. And, sadly, from today onwards, you.'

'I don't want it. It's yours, take it and go.'

'It's too late. Whether or not you want it, you're mixed up in this now. So it would be better for you to wipe those tears away and keep an eye out for people coming.' I take a clean tissue out of my pocket and hold it out to her. 'I'm getting out now. It's almost stopped raining.'

I take the rope out of the boot, stand at the foot of the post, and as close as possible to the bas, put one end under a stone that I pull out of the clay: in the hole that is left, an irregular semicircle, dark and damp, two worms are woken from their lethargy. To start with I think about taking the spade with me, and have even taken it out of the boot, but then I realise that with the spade (carrying it in one hand, under my arm, or over a shoulder) it will be difficult to unroll the rope. So I leave it nearby, leaning against the post, sunk a little into the ground, near the worms, which are still wound up together. The best thing for me to do, I think, is concentrate to start with on the rope. I'll have time to come back for the spade. Behind the Land Rover's windscreen, her eyes still wet, Mirta is paying more attention to my indecisive musings, which are probably quite disconcerting, than she is to watching the road.

I start to unroll the rest of the rope while walking, with much more care than should normally be spent on actions of this kind, under the rain, which has grown heavier. You have to weigh up every release, every pace, every tug: the ground is a swamp of mud and the slightest slip on my part would mean pulling the rope out from under its rock and ruining the attempt. In fact, when I have gone a few paces, no more than ten, I look back and see that the end of the rope has slipped out from under the stone and is following me as if it were the tail of a rough-skinned and woven serpent. I head back and pick up the loose end, but this time, under the moist (and slightly incredulous) gaze of Mirta (whom I sense rather than see behind the occasional sweep of the windscreen wipers), I tie the end, already a little frayed, to the post with a solid knot. The rain falls vigorously on my hands, as I, bent double, pull the rope towards my chest, trying the knot again and again. This time, I murmur. This time, I say out loud as I walk with a firm step along the muddy edge of Mirta's fence. And I am speaking the truth, as each time I look back I see the rope still attached to the post through the curtain of rain. Mirta's face, is now only a pale image, out of focus and irregularly wiped away by the Land Rover's little brushes.

I go through the gate, with the house in the background spurting water off its eaves, and on the next loop in the rope I see the mark the chandler made when he sold it to me. One more turn and the first part of the journey is complete and the rope stretches out in a straight line, more or less, on the mud. The time has now come to turn ninety degrees to the right, to slide the rope under the fence, cross over and carry on unrolling it, and that is what I do.

The last few feet of rope unfold parallel to the row of dolphins. I only have six or seven twists of rope round my elbow and, as I imagined, my previous thoughts seem to be proved right; the rope will not reach the house. I have a margin of three or maybe four feet to play with. It turns out to be slightly more than three, and as I head back for the spade, covered in mud and water, I smile, or maybe I retain a grimace approximating satisfaction on my face, or it could be an impassive but self-satisfied rictus. Mirta lifts her right hand, and I raise my left, hoick my chin at her and put the shovel on one shoulder before heading back inside the fence.

The spade sinks easily into the earth, with hardly any resistance. In a few minutes there is a hole at my feet and a pile of earth to my right: earth and stone on earth and stone. I try to widen the edge of the hole, but all that happens is that the bottom of the hole fills up with rain. The rope, I think, might have got twisted at some point and I might be digging in vain, in one of the infinite number of places in the world where the money is not buried.

I put the spade down and retrace my steps. Everything is fine, or at least seems to be: the rope is stretched out; the angle of ninety degrees is perfect; the post is in its place, with the rope knotted round it. Then I have an idea: it's the post. That must be it. I've wasted two or three feet of rope tying the end to the post, but I haven't taken that detail into account in my calculations. So I am digging in the wrong spot, two or three feet in front of the x on my map. I take up the spade again and sink it deep into the earth. One shovelful. Another. Another. And so on until the shovel hits the black plastic where the haul is wrapped up. I sink to my knees and shout out in joy, but then I feel ashamed without knowing very well why, perhaps for Ed, for Harry, for poor Þóra, who still will be refusing to accept that I am dead.

Back at the car, I concentrate on dividing the bounty into two heaps, one on each leg, as Mirta watches me. The Argentinian takes hers and takes her leave with a long, damp and unexpected kiss on the lips. '*Sos lindo*', she says in her language and then gets out of the car. I watch her leave and spend a good while rubbing my thumb over my moustache, with the motor running in the Land Rover and my half million on my lap. It is raining heavily, as it did on the evening before, when for a few moments London went dark. The rain is falling so insistently that the wipers are barely strong enough to clear the water away.

6. [TRIANGLE]

CROTONE

CROTONE IS ON THE EAST COAST OF CALABRIA, FACING THE Ionian Sea. The legend states that Crotone derives from the giant Kroton, son of Aeacus, who was condemned by the gods never to find peace until he had founded a magnificent city. Of course, that must have happened a while before the *'ndràngheta** turned up.

The Vacalebres have never belonged to the *'ndràngheta*, and I am proud of that. This is not to say that I think that the *'ndrine†* would only accept treacherous schizophrenics who would be happy to kill their mothers for a gram of heroin. Not

---

* The *'ndràngheta* is one of the chief Italian mafia organisations, along with the *cosa nostra* in Sicily, the *camorra* in the Campanile and the *sacra corona unita* in Puglia. (*Author's Note.*)

† Mafia clans. (*Author's Note.*)

at all. The *'ndrine* consist of normal men and (very few) women, who look like us.

The statistics say that if you put four people from anywhere in Calabria in a room, then at least one of them would be somehow or other involved in a *cosca*[*]. So no one could be surprised that throughout my childhood in Crotone I meet and play with and even eat with and stay at the house of various children from *famiglie*[†]. Don't think for a moment that I'm referring to big flashy mansions, like in the American movies. I'm talking about flats with three or four bedrooms and a bathroom, that open onto a patio, where there's a television always on and an electric heater and an oven in the kitchen as the chief indicators of modernity.

Out of all the children of Mafiosi, I spend most time with and am closest to the Facchineris. The first time I see Bruna and Francesco Facchineri, Francesco has his sister sitting on his lap in the back seat of a golden-yellow *cinquino*[‡], both of them hedged in by an endless quantity of suitcases and trunks, looking out of the window at the life of the Via Panella: extravagant balconies sticking out of recently plastered facades, huddles of women walking down the street and a dog or two, lost and languid.

The Facchineris had bought the house that the Panuzzis used to own; they had left Crotone barely an hour before, so the chances of the two families meeting en route (either passing each other on the motorway, or in a bar or a petrol station)

* Criminal group related to the mafia. (*Author's Note.*)
† Mafia families. (*Author's Note.*)
‡ Fiat 500. (*Author's Note.*)

are pretty high. Over the last few years Salvatore Panuzzi, one of the Reggio Panuzzis, had spent all his time collecting the *tangente*§, and now it is likely that the new tenants will take over this lucrative responsibility. I imagined Salvatore getting out of his car on the hard shoulder and handing surreptitiously a handwritten list to his replacement through the window of the *cinquino*, or else I also imagined that this could take place elbow to elbow in a municipal lavatory, while both of them urinated or pretended to do so, and the water ran and the cisterns gurgled.

However the transfer of power took place, my father, Cosimo Vacalebre, and our bakery must surely have appeared on the list. When I was still a young girl, my father resisted this extortion, and if I cast my mind very far back, then I can remember him, with a black eye and his head wrapped in bandages, tiptoeing across past my bed in order to have one last look at the shop through the blinds before heading to his own bed. Other people took the same rebellious path as my father. They spoke of a secret alliance ready to use the mafia's methods against them, but this was before little Orsino, the youngest son of Anselmo the cobbler, disappeared, and a few days later his mother received, wrapped in a paper aeroplane, the kid's left ear. After that, life returned to its normal routine, deaf dumb and blind as ever.

Bruna and Francesco Facchineri, the children I've told you about, came to my classroom the next day during the middle

§ Also known as the *pizza* or the *mazetta*, the *tangente* is the percentage taken by the mafia from the earnings made by businessmen, manufacturers and public sector workers. (*Author's Note.*)

of a nature study lesson. They came holding hands with their mother, Benvenuta, a short woman with black curly hair. Francesco, Bruna, she said after she had finished making the last adjustments to her daughter's plaits, say hello to Miss Maldovani and sit where she tells you to. I'm sorry we're late, she adds, but we got here late yesterday and I still haven't had time to unpack and organise the house. Come on children, shake hands with your teacher, what are you waiting for?

The teacher puts her arm round Bruna's shoulders and takes her to the empty desk next to mine, in the third row. Then she goes back from Francesco and sends him to the back of the class, with the other boys. The kid stumbles on a broken tile in the floor and there are a few little ripples of laughter that the teacher immediately silences. He's clumsy, Bruna whispers into my ear. He thinks he's very clever, but he's clumsy, she murmurs. Their mother, with a cigarette unlit between the fingers of her right hand, stands with her back to the blackboard, in front of the picture of a cow's stomach that the teacher drew in coloured chalk at the beginning of the class. When Francesco is in his place, Benvenuta blows a kiss at him and another one to Bruna, which her daughter returns. Then she puts her long-nailed hands into a black leather bag, takes out a cheap lighter, lights the cigarette and leaves the room. You can hear her heels clicking for a while along the passage that leads to the patio and the street. And then there is silence. A cow's stomach has four parts, the teacher continues, the rumen, reticulum, omasum, and abomasum.

At first sight, Benvenuta Facchineri does not seem to me to be a stereotypical mafia wife, and really, to tell the truth, now that two decades have gone by, I still don't think that she was. A little rough, perhaps, no point not admitting it, but not malicious, and with a certain, slightly rustic, refinement. Much worse women have walked down the Via Panella, such as Salvatora and Sofia Stasi for example, whom I find it easy to imagine washing the blood and shit out of their husbands' clothes after a debtor got strangled, or a sneak got a bullet between the eyes.

However, whether they be refined or crude, over time, yesterday or today, it is inevitable that women find out their husband's criminal secrets. This, the fear that they will reveal these secrets, and no other reason is why the 'ndrangheta can't allow themselves to have women dislike them, and in fact generally allow them a free rein in the private sphere of family life. Women, and Benvenuta would not be an exception to this norm, are the ones who maintain the essence of the mafia: they tell their children to look up to and admire their fathers, who spend a large part of their life away from home (behind bars, usually), and, as if that were not enough, they often lend their names as cover for their husbands' illicit business and shady deals.

The first morning I take bread to the Facchineri's house, the day after Benvenuta and her children turn up at school, it is pouring with rain and the Ionian Sea is turbulent with waves. I have kept the bread dry by putting it under my jersey; by the time I ring the bell, my shoes are soaking and rivulets of water run from my wet hair down my forehead and cheeks. Through the door I can hear the final chords of *E lucevan le stelle*, from *Tosca*. Of course, I only know this much later (that it's a song and that it comes from the opera *Tosca*). At this point *E lucevan le stelle* (Cavaradossi's aria) is just an unknown melody; the saddest and most affecting music I have heard in my life: *Svanì per sempre il sogno mio d'amore... / L'ora è fuggita... / E muoio disperato! / E muoio disperato! / E non ho amato mai tanto la vita! Tanto la vita!* is how the last lines run.*

The door opens a little and Benvenuta appears in stages. She is barefoot, dressed in a white nightdress out from under which stick the bright red nails of her feet.

'Bread,' I say.

'Are you the girl who sits with Bruna?'

I nod.

'Come on, come in, don't stay out there,' she says. The rain is getting heavier. 'Give me that and take off those shoes and that jersey straight away. You're soaked. Bruna,' she calls above the music, 'your friend has brought the bread, lay a place for her at the table.'

'Which friend?' I hear someone asking Bruna.

I walk down the entrance hall behind Benvenuta and, while she puts my shoes and jersey in front of the electric heater, I go into the dining room.

'Ah, it's you, Adina,' Bruna says when she sees me. 'Come on, come and sit with us.'

The floor is covered with a greenish carpet and I still feel the rain under my feet. As I head over to the fold-out table, set up in front of a window down which the rain is gushing, I feel

---

* My dream of love disappears for ever... / The hour has passed... / And I die despairing! / And I die despairing! / And I have never loved life so much! Life so much! (*Author's Note.*)

as if I am walking on grass. *Tosca* is playing on a record player on a shelf, next to a pile of records, and Bruna, Francesco and Damiano, the children's father, are dunking cake into cups of steaming hot chocolate.

'So you are Adina Vacalebre, the baker's daughter,' Damiano says. His voice is deep and a little harsh and there is a strange whistling noise as he breathes, as if someone had left a gas tap on. In his pyjamas he's no different from other men.

'Yes,' I burble.

'Tomorrow,' he says, 'as soon as I get a couple of things in order, I'm planning to go and introduce myself to your father.'

Benvenuta comes back into the room with a cup in her hand and places it in front of me on top of the Spiderman oilcloth that covers the whole table. This cloth reproduces, in an infinite number of identical images, a foreshortened superhero climbing the glass front of a skyscraper. In the glass, like a ghost, his face is reflected, a spiderweb against a bright red background.

'Drink up,' she says, 'you'll feel better.'

'Yes, drink slowly,' Bruna says. 'We've still got time before we need to be at school.'

On the other side of the window the rain is still falling in thick drops, and it will continue for the next few hours. The only thing that will change is the window: first of all the rectangular window of the Facchineri's dining room, then the large windows of the schoolroom, and finally the window of my bedroom. The rain does not stop all morning, and carries on falling throughout the afternoon and most of the night as well. Crotone looks like a postcard of Venice, and the Ionian

Sea is so close to the city that the waves come up to the doors of the houses by the harbour. The flood comes about a foot up on shop fronts and ground-floor flats, and men and women, in water up to their knees, try to save as much as they can and push the water and the mud out of their houses.

Our bakery has also suffered from the rain. Dozens of floppy loaves, onion bread, olive bread, bread with peppers, with cheese, with sage are all floating in the dirty water. The flour from a broken sack has mixed with the water and formed, behind the counter, a lumpy ashen clay that it is very difficult to walk over. Father shovels the mud in huge spadesful out into the street, where a number of doughnuts are now blocking the drains; meanwhile, mother and I throw the water out in buckets. I narrowly miss throwing one of these buckets over Damiano Facchineri, who, dressed in an impeccable cyan suit and with the water lapping at his calves (standing up he is a very tall man), is just about to come in.

'Have you even heard of manna, Adina?' he asks me with a smile. His right hand holds my chin for a moment.

'No, I haven't,' I reply.

'It's a story from the Bible.' Damiano Facchineri sinks into silence for a moment and his laboured, whistling breath suddenly seems to mean something. Then he continues. 'God asks Moses to take his people through the desert. Men, women and children walk under the sun for three long days, and then, very thirsty, they see a pool in the distance. They run over to it, but as soon as they start to drink they realise that the water is bitter. They are upset and turn on Moses, who, using a piece of wood he finds by the pool, fans the wood and calls on divine aid. The water then turns sweet and delicious.' Facchineri pauses here to adjust his tie, a narrow chewing-gum-coloured piece of fabric, reminiscent of a lizard's tongue. 'Days later,' he continues, 'the people are getting unhappy again. They've got nothing to eat, so Moses asks God for help once more. This time God gives them meat at night-time, and makes it rain bread in the mornings, manna from heaven. And so it goes, day after day, for forty years. It is a gift. People don't have to work for it or offer anything in return. All they have to do is take their daily bread and eat it. To begin with the people are joyful, but then the first complaints start up, there are people who start to hate manna, find it disgusting.'

Facchineri stops his story all of a sudden. Father has just come out from behind the counter and, holding the shovel tightly, he approaches with short steps.

'Why are you telling my daughter this?' he asks.

Mother also comes out to see what is happening. Her eyes are wide open, but tired, and the tip of her nose has a smudge of mud on it.

'No reason,' Damiano says, 'I just wanted to explain to your daughter that God gives manna as well as taking it away. This flood is really dreadful.' Father agrees reluctantly. 'My name is Damiano, Damiano Facchineri, and, if you are willing, I'd like to help you clear all this up. I'll help you today; you'll help me tomorrow. You know how it is.'

For a few moments Father looks down at the mud. Then he says:

'There's another shovel indoors, you can get it if that's what you want. We could do with another pair of hands.'

'Here they are,' Damian murmurs. And as soon as he says this, he puts his hands on his chest. They are thin but strong, with pinkish nails.

Damiano Facchineri helps us for a few hours, and when everything is more or less in order, he leaves humming the last few bars of *E lucevan le stelle* and heads to the next-door fishmonger run by Settimo Cosido, around which, in a thick stinking pool of mud and scales, dozens of fish are floating belly upwards. It has been several minutes by now, maybe half an hour, since Facchineri has taken off his jacket and shirt, and now he has both articles tied round his waist by the sleeves like a student on an unseasonably hot winter's day. Now, while he (like a flagpole in a battlefield) stands stranded in the mud talking to Settimo and offers him, gesticulating, help, his torso is only covered by a striped t-shirt spattered with dirt, which leaves uncovered a prison tattoo on his right biceps. It is the red and black face of a man without a mouth, his eyes wide open, behind the bars of a jail cell. Settimo, along with father, mother and me, find it difficult to take our eyes off the tattoo. Settimo's eyes, for all that they try to move away, find it difficult to look anywhere else. Even in his struggle against the mud, once he has accepted Facchineri's help, Settimo seems to have lost a little liveliness: he throws the odd half empty shovelful of dirt towards the horizon or else throws a dead fish into a box almost by pure inertia, all the time never allowing his eyes to stray far away from the tattoo. The same happens with Anselmo Greco who, the tattoo right in his face, is stunned, struck dumb, just like one of the shoes, boots or slippers that float out of his shop and are shipwrecked without their pairs all along the Via Panella.

The story as I've just told it takes place at around the beginning of the month and the shopkeepers don't hear anything else from Facchineri until the start of the next month. This is when the *sgarrista** goes round all the shops in Crotone all day to collect the *tangente*, but from what I hear mother and father muttering about here and there, the system of collection is very different from that of his predecessor, Salvatore Panuzzi. Facchineri doesn't ask for a fixed sum each month, but instead demands a percentage, five per cent of the profits, and if there aren't any profits, he emphasizes, arching his eyebrows (I imagine him arching his eyebrows), then you don't have to pay anything. In practice, this is a model based on trust, and of course, he warns, any attempt to cheat could result in undesirable consequences (here I imagine him twisting his lower lip, perhaps putting his hand, with its pretty pink nails on top of the tattoo underneath his recently-ironed cyan jacket). As return for the payments, Facchineri talks about various benefits: anti-robbery insurance, low-interest loans (at rates lower than those of the banks), new clients (press-ganged, doubtless), and so on. In any case, this is an agreement, he insists, and as such, one is free to accept or refuse the conditions as one wishes: the manna falls every dawn—he explains, stretching up his hands to the sky (or at least this is how father imitates him)—it can

* The mafioso whose job it is to collect extortion money and commissions. (*Author's Note.*)

carry on falling for hundreds, thousands of years, but no one is obliged to pick it up.

Facchineri comes for the *tangente* every month. He holds out his hand with its pink nails, takes whatever the shopkeeper offers him, folds the notes with a soft crackle (the same kind as he has when he breathes) and puts them quickly into the inside pocket of his jacket. Never, whatever the amount he is given, does he ask questions or ask for the account books or the invoices (and no one complains about this). Even in the months when old Andrea, the mother of Settimo Cosido, is hospitalised for a stroke, Facchineri demands his contribution of the fishmonger. Day by day the *sgarrista* gains in presence and impartiality: if a window is shattered by a ball or a stone, then Facchineri, in his clean cyan suit, will appear in a few hours holding by the arm a tearful child ready to ask forgiveness and work until he's paid off his fault. If someone is late paying the baker's bill, or the fishmonger's, or the repair of a pair of slippers, then Faccineri will offer to give them a quick visit (just a recommendation, as he himself says), and the matter is brought to a conclusion. The last Friday of each month, halfway through the afternoon, Facchineri will go to the school with his record player under one arm and put it on Miss Maldovani's table. He plugs it un at the plug under the blackboard, sticks a record of some Puccini opera on the turntable (*Madame Butterfly*, *La Bohème*, *Turandot*, *Manon Lescaut* or the inevitable *Tosca*), carefully positions the needle and, with Bruna sitting on his lap, sits next to me to listen. He is not the only adult who is not a teacher to come to the school. Ever since they set up a Parents' Association, a parent comes every week to school to tell us about his job. My father, for example, mixes a *panettone** before our very eyes and covers it with a crunchy layer of almonds. He also makes *stracette*[†] and *turditti*[‡] and fills a tray of cakes with cream and sprinkles sugar on top of them. For his part, once his mother is out of hospital, Settimo Cosido comes into the school one morning with a swordfish on his shoulder and, after placing it, large and bright and slippery as it is on Miss Maldovani's desk, starts to cut it up. He chops off its head and its tail with solid blows from his sharp machete, guts it, disdainfully throws away the soft, sticky and dripping guts into a copper bucket, then chops the meat into slices. Anselmo, the cobbler, shows us how to fit a boot into a last, and how to fix a heel properly, while little Orsino, with his single ear and his feet stuffed into the hanger for paper aeroplanes that is his desk, hangs on every word of his father's explanation. We also get, filing through the classroom, a waiter, an electrician, a builder, a *carabiniero*, a points man and a doctor with a long white bushy beard, out from under which shyly peeks the rubber tube of a phonendoscope. The doctor, who asks us to call him by his surname, Creazzo, is about to press the bell of this instrument to Francesco Facchineri's heart and lungs when Benvenuta rushes into the class.

'He's dying!' she screams. 'Damiano is fading fast.' Francesco rushes away from the bell of the phonendoscope and hugs his mother, who seems older without her makeup and who wears

---

* Italian sweet that is notable for its intense flavour, both clear and aromatic, and its exquisite combination of dried fruit and sugar. (*Author's Note.*)

† Traditional Calabrian biscuits. (*Author's Note.*)

‡ Sweets made of pasta and aniseed. (*Author's Note.*)

her hair in a tight black ponytail. Bruna gets up from her desk and, her plaits knocking together as she runs, hurries towards them.

'Calm down and tell me exactly what is happening to your husband,' Creazzo asks. He is trying to gain some time while he puts away the tools (a sphygmomanometer, a rusted reflex hammer and the aforementioned phonendoscope), which have been on Miss Maldovani's desk up until this moment.

'It's horrible, doctor,' Benvenuta replies, 'he's finding it impossible to breathe and his lips and his fingernails have gone blue.'

Creazzo nods and forcefully zips up his bag. Then, with Benvenuta and her two children following him, he leaves the classroom with quick steps, leaving a worried murmur behind him.

Minutes later Facchineri is admitted to the San Giovanni di Dio hospital suffering from cyanosis (whose main symptom is that the skin turns bluish because of the blood receiving insufficient oxygen) and four or five days later, when the relevant tests have been carried out, he is diagnosed with heart trouble. The patient stays for almost a week under observation, in one of those green hospital shifts that leaves the legs and the buttocks exposed, and which is tied at the back with a thin cord. Once this period is over, he heads up to the fifth floor, a square room with a black and white television that needs tokens to work, where his treatment with vasodilators and diuretics is continued. There is a large window in one of the walls, out of which Benvenuta breathes the smoke of her cigarettes and from which one can see three quarters of the stands and the pitch of Ezio Scida, F.C. Crotone's home ground. On match days, Facchineri is visited by other patients who, in pyjamas or in their green hospital shifts, walk slowly from their rooms (on crutches, bandaged or even with their drips attached) in order to see the game.

A long way from the hospital and the turf of the Ezio Scida, in the Via Panella, the *sgarrista*'s illness causes a deal of worry among the shopkeepers, who all meet in the bakery at my father's request. On the one hand, no one knows how bad Facchineri's situation is. Doctor Creazzo, who could have explained everything, has gone to Rome, where he is due to attend a conference on family medicine, and he has not left a phone number or an address where a telegram could reach him. Some afternoons Benvenuta leaves Bruna and Francesco in our house when they come out of school so that she can go to the hospital, but she is not a very forthcoming woman and the children don't know all that much: all they know (and all they repeat), they have heard from their mother, which is that their father will be back to normal sooner rather than later. This could be a single isolated attack, or else a chronic illness that renders Facchineri unfit to carry out his job: this last is the general opinion. The idea of being under the protection of a man of delicate health is not pleasant to anyone. In such a condition it is possible that new *bubas* (for such was the name Settimo Cosido gave them) would appear, little unfocussed wicked kids who were on close terms with general delinquency. Or, and this is an even more alarming suggestion, so Anselmo Greco and my father agreed, another representative of the *'ndrangheta* might take over the Via Panella for himself, and leave them, at least for a time, without knowing who to deal with. In the end, if you compared him with other people (his predecessor Salvatore Panuzzi, among others), who would have tarred and feathered their own grandmothers for a fistful of lire, then Facchineri was almost a virtuoso. So, the most intelligent thing to do for the time being, they decide, is to find out exactly what Facchineri's state of health is.

A delegation goes to the hospital. Most of the men, dressed in their Sunday suits, surround Facchineri's bed and fill his room with anxious murmuring, but some of them go straight to the window and even cross themselves before taking a look at the hallowed turf of F.C. Crotone. Settimo, with his hands behind his back, acts as the group's spokesman:

'We have brought you something,' he explains, and then displays and holds out to Facchineri, who seems to be a pale and bony mannequin inside his green hospital shift, a package well wrapped up in gold paper.

The *sgarrista* says a modest thank you, and with his eyes half closed, holds the package on the outstretched palm of his left hand. He is leaning back on a pillow that is twisted and wrinkled, with vanilla-coloured drool on the edges; and out from his right arm, a few centimetres underneath the tattoo in red and black of the mouthless man behind bars (the tattoo which sooner or later becomes the object of everyone's gaze), a transparent plastic tube connects him to a bag of saline solution.

'Thank you,' he whispers once again, and while he tries to focus his inexpressive eyes on the golden packet, eyes which seem to have forced their way out of a haggard and angular face, he points his chin at Settimo to show that he should open the package. It is the day of evening training, and outside a vigorous voice shouts precise instructions at the Crotone players. Sometimes there is also the sound of a whistle, and voices, laughter and complaints. The shopkeepers are in general more aware of what is happening on the field than what is happening in the room.

Settimo tears away the paper and brings the present close to Facchineri's face so that he can see it with clarity. It is a record, and when the patient sees on the label, against a blue background and wearing a heavy jewelled necklace, the cold Greek beauty of Maria Callas as Tosca, he takes the record in his hands. Callas, Carlo Bergonzi, Tito Gobbi, Leonardo Monreale, he reads out in a low voice, his face sketching a tragicomic grimace that in normal circumstances would almost be a smile. Paris National Opera, 1965. Thank you, thank you very much, he repeats, but his voice is almost inaudible among the whistles and the voices coming from Ezio Scida, which are more intense and more urgent with each passing minute. To take the record out of its case, the Mafioso pulls at the edge of the vinyl. He takes it completely out, and suddenly, from the inside of the case, several bundles of lire tied with rubber bands fall to the sheet. The bundles, which are very thin, bounce on the white terylene sheet and most of them fall onto the white tiled floor. No need, friends, Facchineri murmurs in his whistling voice. Really, no need, he says and shakes his head while some of the men, Settimo among them, bend down to pick up the money and look for some space among the sheets to place it.

Things don't work like this, Facchineri insists as my father holds out a sealed envelope. Between this meeting and the previous one, the shopkeepers' visit to the hospital, more than two months have gone by and the *sgarrista* seems recovered. He has changed his cyan suit for a pearl-grey one, light and festive as a heron's plumage, and the cheery May sun pours under the door of the bakery and shines lemony light on the tips of his shoes. Benvenuta said, he continues, that you Vacalebres spent a lot of time looking after Francesco and Bruna while I was in the hospital. I just came to say thank you, so keep your envelope.

'No problem,' my father says, 'but I didn't do it for money. So take your envelope and go. I've got work to do.'

Facchineri takes the envelope and without opening it tears it into pieces, which fall onto the floury cement floor.

'I don't need your money, Vacalebre,' he says. 'I can come and take it whenever I want. I can take everything I want: this bread, your house, this whole neighbourhood if I want...'

'I remember: manna.'

'Don't forget it.'

This conversation takes place early in the morning, while Benvenuta is hanging some flowery sheets from the window, and Francesco and Bruna and I are waiting to go to school and flicking through some magazines on top of the Spiderman oilcloth. A few minutes later, as soon as we are out in the street, we are stopped by an elderly man and a young man aged about twenty. They are both dressed sombrely, in black suits with black shoes and ties.

'Are you Damiano's children?' the older man asks.

Francesco, hesitant and prim, nods, and then specifies that I am not a part of the family, and immediately gets an elbow in the side from Bruna.

'Don't worry, kiddo, I'm a friend of the family and this strapping young man is my son.' The younger man smiles and closes his caramel brown eyes. A thin moustache navigates his lips like a birchbark canoe. 'But you're right, I think your brother shouldn't go around talking to strangers. Is that what your father taught you?' Bruna shakes her head and her braids bounce against the brown leather satchel she carries with a couple of straps like a rucksack. 'No, I don't think that Damiano would tell his children to be trusting. That's not like him. You seem to be very sensible, kiddo. I'll talk to you. I want to show you something.' The man rolls up the sleeve of his jacket and shows a tattoo on his forearm: the red and black face of a man without eyes, his mouth wide open, behind the bars of a cell. At first sight the tattoo might be the same as Facchineri's but it is not. His tattoo has no mouth and this one has no eyes. Also, in this one the bars are rigid, unbent. 'There was a time when your father and I were very close to each other,' the man says in the face of our expressions of surprise. 'And now it would be best if you ran along. I don't want you to be late to school because of me.'

It's a sunny morning; there are only a few clouds like patches on the sky. In the distance, as we walk the cobbled road to school, the waters of the Ionian enter and leave the breakwater with an unusual looseness. Francesco is still annoyed about the elbow in the ribs, so he doesn't speak to Bruna. I try saying the first thing that comes into my head, that we will soon be able to go swimming after class, or that the blackberries are getting ripe on the brambles, but all I get in return is a shrug of the shoulders and silence, silence above all. The school is at the end of the route: a brick cube with windows patching it at intervals. They say that nearby, or maybe even on this arid broken land, Pythagoras built his school of mathematics more than two thousand years ago. One of his disciples, Milo of Crotone (a local hero) was a famous wrestler and triumphed at several Olympic Games, and has unlikely feats attributed to him, such as being able to stop a cart that was pushed towards him at top speed, or else being able to hold a bull on his shoulders. Miss Maldovani is from Rome, and when she gets angry she normally says with a deep sigh that the history of Crotone repeats itself year after year: not enough Pythagorases and too many Milos.

But today she seems in a good mood. She has just used several colours of chalk to paint the various layers of the atmosphere (troposphere, stratosphere, mesosphere, ionosphere and exosphere), and now she is using white chalk to indicate, in round and legible numbers, the height of each layer. She is just about to finish the task (all she has left to do is to close the final zero of the 2,000 kilometres of the exosphere) when the door bursts open and Facchineri comes into the room with long strides. Urgently, he goes to Francesco's desk and then to the one that Bruna and I share and takes his children by the hand and drags them towards the door. His suit is so white and so large, and he comes so quickly, that it is as if his children are being snatched by a shining light. When he reaches the door, the *sgarrista* calls to Miss Mantovani that he does not have time to explain, but that she shouldn't worry, it's nothing serious. She holds the chalk in one fist and seems to grow smaller in front of the blackboard, she stands underneath the mesosphere shrunk into her grey sleeveless dress with its black cloth belt and large red buckle. The sun shines on her with a saffron-coloured light, and she throws a long shadow onto the floor. When the final murmurs that this sudden entrance and departure have caused die away, Maldovani turns to the class and says:

'The troposphere is the lowest layer of the atmosphere, but also the most important: life is only possible within it.' She turns back and points to the board with her chalk. 'As you can see, it extends from the earth's surface to an altitude of eighteen kilometres.' She turns back. The sun hits her belt buckle and refracts in ruby-coloured light. 'The troposphere is also the most unstable part of the atmosphere,' she continues, 'because it is where all the weather takes place, and it is where aeroplanes fly, although sometimes, to avoid problems, they move through the stratosphere. Orsino,' she says, pointing with the chalk, 'you like aeroplanes so much, have you ever been in one? Better, why don't you raise your hands all of you who have ever been in an aeroplane.'

Facchineri's *cinquino* is parked in front of his house with the boot open. Benvenuta opens the door straight away as soon as I ring the bell. Her lips and her fingernails and her toenails are painted with that intense red that makes them seem so much bigger, and her hair is in rollers and covered in a net.

'Bruna can't come out to play,' she says quickly. 'We're going. We're going to another city,' she explains. 'But if you want to you can come in and say goodbye.'

There are suitcases, trunks, bundles and packages piled up in heaps in the entrance, and Damiano and Francesco, scarcely looking at me, bring more and more objects from the living room, the kitchen and the bedrooms. The only things that are familiar here are the Spiderman cloth and the record player, where *Tosca* is playing at a low volume, almost inaudible under this domestic upheaval. Bruna is sitting cross-legged on the green carpet, organising the paints in her paintbox.

'I'll write to you when we get to Catania,' she says with a smile. 'Daddy says that we'll go across the straits of Messina in a ferry. It will be very pretty.'

'I'm sure it is,' I say.

And as soon as I say this I hear the whistling noise of a pistol shot, followed by a shout and another shot. I grab Bruna by one arm and drag her with me under the table, away from the paintbox. I cover her mouth with my hand. Don't speak and don't move, I whisper. The Spiderman cloth reaches almost down to the floor, but there is a little space left open, five centimetres through which there filters a sulphurous light into the shadows. If anyone bends down or goes on their knees, they'll be able to see our feet. There are more shots, footsteps, blows, the noise of objects and bodies falling, shouting, pleas, tears: voices that I find it hard to identify in the middle of all the hullabaloo. The air smells of gunpowder. Bruna is trembling from her head to her toes, shuddering, finding it difficult to breathe. Her eyes are filled with tears which, dropping silently, fall down her cheeks and wet my hand: If I take my hand away, the most likely thing is that she'll burst out into uncontrollable tears. A car starts up. We hear it going away until the noise is a distant and mechanical purr. The only thing I can hear is the air reluctantly entering Bruna's lungs, then suddenly the first bars of *E lucevan la stelle* are audible: *E lucevan la stele / ed olezzava la terra / strideo l'uscio dell'orto / e un passo sfiorava la rena**. I take my hand away from her mouth, lift the oilcloth, and come out from under the table. I stand on tiptoe and take the needle off the record.

'Wait for me here,' I say to her. 'I'll be back soon.'

Benvenuta's corpse is in the kitchen. It's lying face downwards in a small and rippled pool of blood which, millimetre by millimetre, is gaining ground on the honey-coloured tiles of the floor, and threatens to head under the sink. Some rollers have come loose from her hair and it is only the net that stops them from falling or rolling in their light plastic way onto the floor. The rest of them are in the hallway: Francesco is by the half-open main door, whose handle is covered in a red stain that looks like the shadow of a piece of popcorn. He is lying on his back. A large tartan suitcase and several other bundles are lying on top of his legs. His eyes are half open and he has two bleeding wounds: one in his left side, out of which there pokes part of his intestine, like a large white creamy insect; and another one, a hole the size of a fist, in the middle of his chest. At the other end of the hallway, underneath a canvas that shows a harbour scene, with fishing boats drawn in pastel

* And the stars shone / and a sweet odour came from the earth / as the garden door creaked / and a footstep was heard on the sand. (*Author's Note.*)

colours, and women mending nets in front of a calm sea, the corpse of the tattooed man lies on top of Damiano. His head is on Damiano's shoulder. The volcanic landscape of brains and guts gives the impression that both of them shot without aiming, without pause. As I go back for Bruna I can's stop thinking about how their bodies will be in the morgue, in adjacent drawers, their tattoos visible to everyone. In the years to come this image will appear regularly in my dreams: the two bodies, blue, their heads shaven; their thoraxes sewn up, the freezing cold; and then the two complementary tattoos, which with the passage of the years have not blurred.

Under the table, curled up, Bruna sobs and trembles like a wounded animal. I hold out my hand to help her get up; I give her my handkerchief as well: her eyes are red and wet (and old, one might say) and there is snot on her hair and face. We have to go, I say.

Bruna looks at me in silence, with an expression which is peculiar to madmen: fixed, hard and inexpressive, holding nothing back, straight at my eyes. I feel that with each new breath that she takes she is asking me for an answer. I look at her for a second (you can only hold a gaze like hers for a second), swallow, and tell her the truth: they are all dead.

Bruna's legs shake, they give the unavoidable impression that she will not be able to stand up for any length of time, but then she keeps her balance, holds herself between my arms, buries her face in my shoulder and starts to cry. It is intense, cut off: a groan, followed by a long silence then a series of short sobs. In the distance, when the sobbing ceases for a moment or else relaxes a little, you can hear the hypnotic wail of the sirens and the voices of the neighbours, alarmed by the gunshots, who stand at the foot of Via Panella and speculate about what might be happening.

We have to go, Bruna, I repeat; although in fact I am unable to take even a single step. If I put one foot forward, the most likely thing is that I will fall flat on my face; both of us will fall onto the green carpet, next to the open paintbox (by the set of sharpened pencils that looks like a miniature rainbow) or else by the table, near the Spiderman oilcloth, like fallen buildings of flesh waiting, helplessly, for some superhero to climb them.

The multiple murder is the main story in the major Italian newspapers and brings a large number of reporters to Crotone who, for several days, say three or four, go up and down the Via Panella looking for gossip and interviews. Settimo Cosido, Anselmo Greco, Miss Maldovani and my own father appear in the newspapers giving their own opinions of the events, testimony born of both horror and relief and which portrays Damiano Facchineri in a pretty good light: the *sgarrista* is presented as an honourable, sensitive and fair man, a man of the Law whose single, human error was to have belonged to the wrong team.

Those days, the police presence increases noticeably throughout the city (it is almost as if there is an officer at every door), and through the doors of the Crotone Central Police Station there pass, as if drawn there by the tide of the Ionian Sea, hundreds of capos, swindlers and small-timers with polite little moustaches and brown eyes, whom Bruna and I have to identify, without really wanting to, at interminable identity parades. The criminal business has gone so far out of control that in the local clothing stores, and in clothing stores the length and breadth of the country, you can find t-shirts with Damiano's tattoo, and that of his killer: the red and black face of a man without a mouth and with his eyes wide open, behind the bent back bars of a jail cell, and the red and black face of a man with no eyes and with his mouth wide open behind a set of intact bars. Also, in an unprecedented musical anachronism, *E lucevan la stelle* gets to the top of the hit parade, beating out *Sapore de sale* by Ennio Morricone with vocals by Gino Paoli. A few months later, Paoli (for existential reasons) will try to kill himself by shooting himself through the heart, and although his life will be saved, the surgeons will find it impossible to remove the bullet from his thoracic cavity, just as it will be impossible for other surgeons, the surgeons of time, to remove or destroy the resentment that the deaths of Damiano, Benvenuta and Francesco has caused in Bruna.

The girl, claimed by no family member, stays in the Crotone orphanage, which she only leaves when the police need her for one of these identity parades. From time to time some middle-class couple with their overcoats under their arms comes into the orphanage to see about adopting her, but Bruna never speaks to them, or if she does, it is only to whisper into the woman's ear, as if sharing a secret, that if they do adopt her then on the first full moon she will take a kitchen knife and kill her and her husband while they sleep. This is the sort of story she tells me when I go to visit her on Sunday afternoons or else when, after much arguing (mother and me against father), she is allowed to come to spend the weekend with us. Over time, these weekends become regular occurrences, and then she starts to come with us for holidays and festival days. These are agitated days, weeks, months and years, Luther King will be killed on the Lorraine Motel balcony in Memphis, the city to which Elvis moved after his childhood in Tupelo; Bruna and I will work out how to fasten our first bras together; Hendrix will start to self-destruct; Neil Armstrong, under a black sky, will tread for the first time on the regolith-covered surface of the moon. Then there will be Watergate, *The Godfather*, *The Exorcist*, and Bruna and I will allow some bad boys to undo our first bras together in the back seat of a Fait 850 Spider while Richie Blackmore's guitar howls from the radio. And suddenly, as if our shared adolescence had been a shortened trailer for a much longer feature, we find ourselves in Milan, sharing a student flat near the Central Station that mummy and daddy pay for, religiously, the first of every month.

It is a torrid morning at the end of spring 1981. Bruna, face down on her bed, is concentrating on a heavy book of Pre-Socratic philosophy, and I am finishing painting my lips in the bathroom, the door half open. I have an interview, a temporary job as an interpreter. That's all I know. I still have a few courses to get through to complete my English degree, but I don't, in my youthful self-confidence, imagine that will be a problem. The meeting is to take place in an attic penthouse, two or three blocks from the Duomo, and it is the client himself, and actor called Gaetano Iabichino, who, it being the maid's day off, stretches out a hairy hand and invites me into his office. He is a very attractive man, a gentleman with nut-brown eyes and a beatific smile, whose smile seems to have been designed on an architect's bench, using compass, set-square and triangle. I have seen his face in some *cuore* magazines, in the hairdresser's or in a doctor's waiting-room. However, now that I have him in front of me, in person, and hear his voice, acid and soft as the pulp of an orange, something—an intuition—tells me that I have seen him before, somewhere else, some other time. Sitting in a black armchair, Iabichino explains to me the situation: he is intending to go on tour in Britain and needs an interpreter to go with him for the press appearances and the rest of the promotion activities, someone who can reproduce his Italian words faithfully in English. He has some knowledge of the language, he explains, as he slides towards the edge of his seat, enough to have learnt the role of Kowalski in *A Streetcar Named Desire* and to have 'given his Stanley' without hearing murmurs of dissent and disapproval from the stalls and the gallery; but he does not feel confident in conversation of uttering more than banalities. The British tour, he continues, will be in a month, when he gets back from the tour which he will be starting tomorrow in Iceland. And so he, placing his hands over a silver locket which is lying on his desk, arranges to see me in a fortnight's time when, he says, he will explain all the details to me.

'You mean I'm hired?' I ask.

'Yes. You are young and pretty and maybe, just maybe, you also understand and speak English perfectly,' Iabchino smiles and for a moment, involuntarily closing his eyes. 'So it would be good if you had a look for your passport. I don't want any last-minute surprises.'

'Don't worry. I'll look for it when I get home. So, I'll see you in a fortnight, alright?' I say.

'Yes, same time as today,' he says, and stands up, stretching a hand over to my side of the table, but I still have to lean over to take it. And it is only then, and I would have preferred not to have seen it, that I see the picture in the open locket: the sinister man with the tattoo next to a kid, the young Gaetano Iabichino (or whatever the hell his name is), back in the day when he had a thin blonde moustache, both of them dressed in black, exactly like on that morning. The only difference is in the background, a dusty crossroads in front of which the father and son stand shoulder to shoulder, making victory signs with their index and middle fingers.

Bruna doesn't want me to go with her, but I insist: someone has to call the police while she points the gun at him, and that person has to be me. The police could do it themselves; it would be enough for us to give them a tip-off and in a few minutes a patrol would be at his flat, ready to put the cuffs on Gaetano Iabichino. But that, Bruna says, would be impersonal. She wants it to be her who gives him the news. She wants their gazes to lock like the blades of a pair of scissors; she wants to see the fear in his eyes and for him to see the spark of hatred in hers. And for me this, given how things started out, is something I can deal with. Bruna is very obstinate, and it took me a lot of conversations to convince her that for her own good, she shouldn't kill him. Her first, impulsive reaction was to hang around outside Iabichino's house that very same day and wait for him to come down, then shoot him in the face. Luckily she did not have a pistol to hand, because if she had had one then she would have carried her threat out without a doubt. These two weeks have been vital for me to dissuade her: he's a young man, famous, attractive, I said. He will suffer in prison. They will make him suffer. He will get thirty or forty years and when he leaves, if it isn't in a coffin, he will have no teeth left and won't remember his own name. But don't let your nerves get to you, I am still murmuring to her days later, while we climb the last flight of stairs up to the attic. You have to be cold, Bruna, cold as he has been for all these years. Don't take the gun out until we're inside. And let me do the talking.

The door to the apartment is ajar at the top of the staircase; a wedge of natural light shines from the opening onto the end of a twisted bannister and a pot with an aspidistra. I walk through the light and press the doorbell with the back of my hand. I ring a couple of times, but no one comes to answer the call and no one shouts out to me to come in or to go back to wherever I came from. The only sound apart from the occasional traffic sound from the cars around the Duomo is a sort of liquid hissing, a running tap or else a cistern filling up. I press the bell for the third and final time (I don't want to alert the neighbours), but with the same lack of result. So I hide my right fist in the sleeve of my shirt, push the golden doorknob just enough to open the door and let us in, and take a few steps into the corridor, stopping in front of a photograph of a volcano erupting, with lava on one side of the picture, and a group of men, women and children protecting themselves from the falling ash under umbrellas on the other. Bruna follows close behind me with her hand in her pocket, holding the handle of the pistol. The main door swings shut behind her (perhaps she closed it or the door closed itself of its own inertia) and suddenly the light, which comes uncomplicatedly out of the open doors to the various rooms of the flat, becomes much more active and whiter. We find the cause of the hissing noise at the end of the corridor: a pool of warm foamy water running out from underneath a door, the only one in the whole house to be closed. The liquid is still spreading; the pool is now as wide as the corridor and is spreading over the parquet. It is over there that we now head, with a hand against each wall so as not to slip. Bruna has the pistol out of her pocket, ready to shoot, and the barrel of the gun precedes us into the room, which turns out to be a large bathroom, with a big mirror mounted over the sink, the walls tiled white, and a huge bath. The hot water tap in the bath has been left open and the water, with a patchy cloud of foam skimming on top of it, laps against the salmon-coloured tiles, falls to the floor in a little cascade and joins the great pool of soapy water on the floor all the way to the door. I go to turn the tap off. My fingers, wrapped in a flannel, are just about to take hold of the silver-plated star of the tap, when I see, under the steam the foam and the water, the naked blue skin of a corpse. I give a little shout, more from surprise than anything else, which Bruna's free hand stops with difficulty.

'It's him, right?' she says, taking her hand away.

I nod.

Bruna throws the pistol into the water with a disdainful gesture, and it bubbles a little and sinks into the space between the man's bony ribs and the side of the bath.

'Are you crazy?' I scold her while, with my arm wet all the way to the elbow, I hunt around in the water until I find the gun under the corpse's buttocks. 'What do you want? Both of us to end up in jail for a crime neither of us has committed?'

'I don't care,' she says. 'At least that way I could get a tattoo like my dad had.' And then, her eyes wet (I don't know if it's because of the disappointment or the steam in the bathroom), she sits (or collapses) on the edge of the bath, next to Iabichino's pale, wrinkled, naked body, which has, as well as rigor mortis, a bloated face, blue lips and a frozen stare.

'He'll understand, Bruna,' I say, to cheer her up. 'Wherever he is, he'll understand that you did the best you could to get revenge. I am sure,' I carry on, with the pistol in my hand, my sleeve still dripping. 'Think about him. Remember how he was, his cyan suit, walking along the Via Panella. Think about something he would say, maybe that will make you feel better.'

We sit still for a couple of minutes in silence, motionless, wreathed in steam. I am about to say that the most sensible thing would be to call the police and get out of there as soon as possible, when Bruna starts speaking:

'Something he would say. "If someone hurts their finger, the safest thing to do is cut off the whole hand,"' she mutters, and her mouth curls a little, the beginnings of a perverse smile.

7. [PARALLELOGRAM]

TWINS

SIT DOWN ON THE SOFA, IF YOU WOULD BE SO KIND. AND DON'T worry about those patterns, just push them to one side. Estela will pick them up when she gets back. She's gone to buy some thimbles, I don't think she'll be too long. I suppose you'll want to talk to her as well. Yes, we are twins, but I'm the elder. I was born ten minutes earlier. Remember it like this: in order to have the ripples, the sea has to be there first.* Yes, that's my name, Mar Sagredo, although I'm so fat that maybe it would be better to call me Ocean. My sister is huge as well, she's not really a ripple, more like a wave. But you have to be careful with her, she doesn't like jokes: she's always in a bad mood and always on a diet. Thyroid problems, you understand. I just really like eating. I could spend the whole day eating, nothing

* The joke here is on the names of the two sisters, Estela [wake, ripple] and Mar [sea].(*Trans.*)

else. So you're a journalist. From *El Correo*. The thing is, we don't really read newspapers. We read celebrity magazines sometimes, you see there's a few around here. We've got them so that the clients can have something to look at while we take their measurements. We don't have time to read ourselves, only every once in a blue moon. We don't stop. I suppose you've come because of the kidnapping. It's been several years, but journalists come almost every month. The other day it was a TV presenter; the poor guy sat down right here, just where you're sitting, right on top of a pincushion. No, don't worry, Estela's put it away by now. The worst that could happen is that you'd sit on a loose needle. Needles get everywhere, that's what they do. Tell me, what is it that you want from us? I was afraid of that: the whole story, all the way from the top. Well, if that's what you want, then we might as well get started. Of course, if you don't mind starting without Estela. Fine, then. You can turn that thing on if you want. Well, it all started when our father died, Heliberto Sagredo. H-E-L-I-B-E-R-T-O. Yes, that's it, the balcony broke and pulled him down as it fell, I see you're aware of all that. So you'll know that my father was immensely fat and that it was his own weight that broke the balcony. So we're all clear up to there. No, this isn't a joke, not at all, unless you want this conversation to be over right now. My father did not kill himself. I'm willing to accept that his own weight killed him, but nothing more. I am very careful with what I say. I warn you that Estela is not as understanding as I am. It's just that my father had split up with my mother at that time, for reasons which don't concern us here. I ask you not to look into that. I've said that he didn't kill himself and I don't want to hear anything else about that topic. Of course, I accept your apology, but don't go down that path. Shortly before my father had his accident, my mother took us home, to our old home, to spend the weekend with him. Dad wasn't going through the best of times, that's for sure. For sure. Nothing more than that, though. I should say that he didn't seem very happy when we turned up suddenly at his door. Yes, he was stressed out by those little rats, the Sincerity League. This is the last time I will say it: he did not kill himself. Maybe he felt threatened by that group of stupid little kids, maybe mother abandoning him had left him devastated, but he did not kill himself. My father was a very level-headed man. So forget about the bloody suicide once and for all. Yes, you are right, I said 'abandoning him'. Separation, divorce, abandonment, who cares. In the end it's always one half of the couple that breaks it. There's always someone who whips away the tablecloth and then keeps it. And now, do you want to continue or shall we leave it here? In that case don't say the word 'suicide' again. Right? Alright. Father's death affected Estela and me a lot, that's clear. One thing is not to see your father for weeks at a time, but it's quite another never to see him ever again. Of course we cried. We cried for a whole week. Mother cried as well. Secretly. Hidden away in her room. Have you ever lost someone who is dear to you? In that case you must know what we felt: emptiness, fear, the sense of being somehow incomplete and knowing you will never be whole again. Smoke if you like. There's an ashtray on the table, next to the magazines, but be careful. This place is full of cloth and will go up like the fourth of July. I said that father's death affected us both a lot, both physically and psychologically. I started to eat a lot. All the time. All roads lead to the fridge. I got fat. I got incredibly fat. I was like a cow. Estela kept on eating the same as before, but she got fat too, unexpectedly. Maybe it was the thyroid, like I said, or maybe it was just solidarity. No, don't look at me like that, twins have a very strongly developed sense of solidarity. If at this very moment, while we are talking, something should happen, God forbid, to Estela, then I would feel pain. We are connected, but the pain would not pass from one of us to the other, but would fill us both. Mind your ash. You're ruining my carpet. I don't know why all you journalists have to smoke, is it in your contract or something? Right, I thought not. It's just a manner of speaking. So, the two of us got fat, like I said, and now that's pretty much irreversible. I am sure, sure as I am of few things, that it was getting fat that made mother take us to a psychologist. His name was (it still is) Teófilo del Toro, and his office was in Bidezabal, in a modern building by the railway. Yes, that's him, 'fortune-teller to the stars', I'm sure that if you open one of these magazines you'll find him straight away. But he's not from Uruguay, don't let the accent fool you, those fizzy 'l's that fade away on the tip of the tongue. Del Toro was born in Pancorbo, the closest village in Burgos as you go away from Bilbao on the motorway. I know that because my mother is from a nearby village, Busto de Bureba, and when they were younger, on days when it didn't snow, they went to the same school. I'll leap ahead a bit now, because as everyone knows it was the waiting room at Teófilo del Toro's consultancy where this whole situation started. Yes, when I say everyone I'm including you as well, but if you want I'll leave you out, make you feel special. I'll tell you, but I thought you'd read something about the case. You're young but that doesn't mean that you don't know how to do your job, of course not. And no, I don't mind at all answering your question. Oh, why am I talking so formally? That's just a habit, comes from spending so much time with customers. You know. Sometimes I'm even super-polite with my own sister. Anyway, I feel more comfortable speaking like this, even if you are younger than me: it's like my mother says, towelling is alright for dressing-gowns, but the bride deserves to wear organdie. What did the waiting-room look like? There's not much to say about that, really. If you've seen one, you've seen them all. A half-lit waiting room with its *démodé* sofas, a grubby Persian rug and in the centre a table with a polychrome rim and two big heaps of magazines on top; and at the back through a thick walnut door, the doctor's office: the desk, the qualifications and graduation photographs framed on the white walls, and a leather divan underneath a window that gives out onto the Arrigunaga beach. But are you going to write an article or a novel? Right, documentation is very important. I understand. I've told you, and if I haven't then I'm telling you now, that everything started in doctor del Toro's consultancy, where all of us women used to meet: Dori Galdearetxe (who was always accompanied by a niece, for mobility issues); Luana Varsavsky; Estela, who must have gone to buy her thimbles in Melanesia, the time she's taking; and me. All of us women, with the exception of doctor del Toro, of course, but it was very unusual for him to come out of his office except to ask the next patient to come through. No, I don't know why Dori and Luana came to therapy every week, I don't think they knew themselves; but if you had seen them as I saw them, then I'm sure you'd have come to your own conclusions in a heartbeat: Dori must have weighed more than two hundred kilos back then, she drove around in a bed on wheels and they had to bring her up to the waiting room in the goods lift. You only had to look at her and you lost your appetite. A man? It could have been. Behind every fat woman there's usually an unhappy love affair, a loss, a void. I know from experience. I know, *vox populi*, that she was married to an Italian actor, Gaetano Iabichino, and that the marriage broke down, that was on the cover of a lot of the magazines, and that then, when she started to let herself go as a woman and as an actress, she had a fling with a police inspector that ended up in nothing. Please, take care. That's the second cigarette in less than half an hour. You should give it up while you still can. Yes, that's what everyone says, and then they don't quit until their lungs have gone black, by which time it's too late. Luana? Poor creature. She was a truly ugly girl, more than two metres tall, and must have been filled with complexes. Every time I think about her I see her bending under the lintel of a door, as if apologising for having got up so high. No, I don't think anyone can talk about guilt in her case. If there is any guilty party, then I suppose it must be nature, human nature: we are cruel to those who are different from us, we spread funny malicious rumours, we laugh out of fear at everything we can't understand, we have to prod other people's wounds. But don't you listen to me; I'm a dressmaker, or a seamstress as they used to call us, a couturier; the talking cure comes from doctor del Toro. Go and speak to him to deal with this kind of question, although I imagine he'll invoke professional privilege and refuse to answer. Also, it won't be easy for you to get in touch with him: he's always very busy. Now, while you and I are chatting, he's probably trying to predict the hair colour of the future great-grandson of some a-lister. He deals with big business. Luana Varsavsky, yes, I hadn't forgotten. Poor little girl. When Luana was a baby, her mother, a single mother to be more precise, took her out of Argentina at midnight one night and flew to London, and when everything was all OK, then the Falklands War broke out and they were all up in the air once again. No, they weren't attacked, but they left as a precaution: they had a couple of threatening phone calls and woke up one morning with graffiti on the front of their house: 'Go home Argentine pigs,' and other pleasantries like that. You know what people are like, and how war makes them worse. Before I forget, did you go to Mirta Varsavsky's exhibition? Yes, the one with all the dolphins. Well, if you truly appreciate art, you should go: it's wonderful. Estela and I were really overwhelmed. You're not comfortable, are you? Don't lie to me. I'll take the patterns off the sofa right away. I thought that my sister would do it when she got back, but she's taking a long time. No, it's no trouble. None at all. I am fat, I don't want to deny it and I can't deny it, but I'm not an invalid. Stay where you are and keep an eye on your cigarette. Better like that, isn't it? Where was I? So, you are in a hurry... No, I'm not a seer like del Toro. I'm saying so because this is the third time in five minutes that you've looked at your watch, and every time you move your wrist the ash falls on the carpet. Please don't attempt to apologise. It's very clear: either a) you don't have very much time, and I can understand that perfectly, or else b) which is much worse, I'm boring you. In any case, a) or b), we need to find a solution we're both happy with. Turn off that thing for a minute and listen closely. If you're fine with it, we can try this: you'll ask me a question and I'll try to answer it. And if you see that I'm not answering or that I'm going on for much too long, then you tell me straight out. Alright? Well, then, press the button. Yes, I could put it like that, it was Dori's idea to begin with, but the real origin, the initial spark, came from the photo album that Luana brought to the waiting room. It was an album from her time at the faculty: Luana had taken the photos at a party to celebrate the beginning of the year. You know: young people all crammed together, euphoric, their shirts untucked and their eyes all red, holding up half-empty plastic cups; in the background the Nervión, or the side of mount Archanda or else the colonnade of the faculty. Psychology. Luana was studying psychology. Odd? I don't think so. I'm sure you smoked lots of cigarettes in secret and read lots of newspapers sitting on the loo before you became a journalist. Well, she did the same, but in a more convenient fashion: went to see a psychologist every Wednesday. I don't see anything odd in that. The key to it all, I'll tell you again, was in the photos, especially one in which a young man knelt down talking (or pretending to talk) to a *katxi** filled with beer. A parody of Hamlet's existential doubts, that's right. I see that you've been

* A *katxi* is a plastic 750 ml glass. *Katxi* is a corruption of *casi* ('nearly'), because the glass holds nearly a litre of liquid. (*Author's Note.*)

looking around. I didn't realise at first, but Estela did. Estela remembered having seen this kid hanging round our house the last weekend we spent with dad. And when Estela said so, I remembered him as well, and then I saw again dad's fat finger pointing down from the balcony, and recall, as if hearing a whisper, my father's large peaceful voice: 'Look, Mar, that one over there, the one who's looking at us and pretending to look in the window of that kiosk, he's one of the bastards who's been insulting me. They think I don't know who they are, and I pretend not to, but I do know them. I've put faces to them all.' Dad might have put a face to this guy, but Luana gave his name: Norberto Fraile. Fraile was the director of the university theatre group, that's in all the archives, and it was precisely this coincidence that inspired Dori to plot a punishment for him. You know, we never even thought about kidnapping them. We were annoyed, upset, yes, I'm not going to deny that, but I've already said that dad didn't kill himself, that it was an accident. That's one thing that my sister and my mother and I have been clear about right from the start. And if you still have even the shadow of a doubt about it, you should ask Estela as soon as she comes through that door. I bet you whatever you like she'll say the same. Yes, please, go ahead and smoke: it's your throat, and your lungs. You don't need to ask my permission every time you light up. Our clients are women and lots of them smoke, they smoke like truckers, I've already said: they smoke while we turn up their hems, or stick them with pins, or measure the armholes. All I do is open the window as soon as they leave, lighting up as they go, usually. As I will do when you leave too. Yes, better to get back to Dori and

Norberto Fraile. Dori used her niece to set up a trap for Fraile, that much is clear. No, we barely knew the niece. I don't think I remember her name, even. Paula or something like that. Laura, that's it, Laura. She helped Dori to get to the consultancy, because of the traffic and so on, but then she would go away and wouldn't come back until the therapy session was over. A boyfriend? It's possible, you know what those 'bobby-soxers' are like. You see them leaving their convent school, glowing with innocence, and then you find them a while later in some dark corner or under a bridge, letting a boy put his hand up their v-neck or down their pleated school skirt. No, don't think it strange that we didn't get on with... Laura, that's it. She must have been about sixteen or seventeen at the time, and we were only twelve. At that age four or five years is almost an abyss. Laura, where were we, yes, Laura was the one who gave Norberto Fraile Dori's number so he could get in touch with her. And this call ended up with them arranging a meeting, with another actor from the university group coming along. This other actor had nothing to do with the harassment of my father, not at all. We can consider him collateral damage. No, I don't know what Dori thought back then about getting an innocent mixed up in all this; to know that you'd have to be able to talk to the dead, and I only do that, talk that is, with the living, and I like it less and less each time I do. What's clear, and there's no two ways about it here, is that the kid ended up getting mixed up in this mess, whether deliberately or by accident, without having anything to do with it. But it wasn't any crime either: Dori had decided to keep Fraile locked in the basement for three or four hours, enough to frighten him a bit and give him what he deserved in the name of all the fatties of the world, and the rest of us (Luana included) thought this was an excellent idea. What happened next was an accident, or better, a series of accidents. Things sometimes happen just because and no one is safe. The sky can suddenly turn black, my father said, and you can get struck by lightning just as you are putting your key into your front door. If my sister had come back by now, the bag of thimbles dangling from her hand, she'd say exactly the same as I do now: there was no ill will, no malice, nothing like that here. Hey: you've put that cigarette out badly, it's still smoking, put it out properly. That's better. No one, and this is the most important point, could have predicted that Dori was going to suffer a sudden heart attack on just that afternoon, just after having locked the boys in the cellar. No, that's not entirely true, sometimes there are no warning signs. I'm not trying to be offensive, just telling you the facts. I'm not a doctor and I never studied medicine, but I am fat, just like Dori was (well, she was much more fat), and fat people, as you might well guess, are predisposed to everything (apart from getting thin). Being fat predisposes me to heart attacks, so I know what I'm talking about. Sometimes there is that squeezing feeling in the chest you mention, that sharp pain; but other times there is not. Other times, there is nothing more than a slight choking feeling, or just excess sweating. Of course we missed Dori in the waiting room, but we didn't think about it very much. It wasn't the first time that she had missed several appointments with del Toro. Dori was unpredictable: she would come regularly for three months, and then suddenly, without any warning, would stop coming for a month or even two. No, there was no public announcement about the boys' disappearance, that much I'm sure of. If Estela or I had seen or heard anything, Estela and I would have got in touch with the police right away. Norberto Fraile's father had (and still has, I imagine) a great deal of money, and the police must have thought that sooner or later there would be a ransom demand. That's why they took so many precautions. The parents of the other child might have been carried along by this excess of zeal. Another one? You know what you're doing, but smoking is a risk factor for heart disease as great or even greater than obesity. Yes, I'm annoying, I know. That's clear. Luana could have noticed Norberto Fraile's absence from the faculty, and Dori's niece could have wondered where her aunt had got to, but I can't really tell you about the closeness of the relations between them. I don't know how often they saw each other or whether the girl did anything more than take Dori to the consultancy. Perhaps, if there were no visits planned to doctor del Toro, they saw each other or spoke on the phone from time to time. You'd have to ask... Laura, that's it. No, better not ask Laura's mother, because she didn't speak to Dori at all. Sisters, what do I know. Luana and Norberto I can tell you about. Listen to me, how many students are there normally in a class at university? About one hundred, right. Well, there's one answer for you right there. And March is an odd month. The kids have just done their mid-term exams, it's not unheard of for them to want to take a break, they go on study trips... Luana spent a long week travelling through Morocco in a double-decker bus with thirty other students. And when she got back she had gastroenteritis. Have you ever tried going over your class list, a list of people you haven't seen for a while, as you throw up and do the other thing as well? I thought as much. Hey, the kid didn't have mental problems. Where did you get that idea from? She was very tall and very ugly, and had serious complexes because of that, but that was all. She slept with a doll, yes, but not just any doll. She slept with Coro, her doll since she'd been a baby. Mad, you say. I should really see your editor and you to get an apology... My father killed himself! Luana was mad! Who knows what you think about me! No, don't apologise, don't put on that butter-wouldn't-melt expression. You're lucky Estela isn't here. I understand, yes, it's part of your job. Yes, alright, stop trying to flatter me and if you want to ask me anything else do it now. I've got things to do. The hand. I knew it. Everyone wants to know about the hand. You're a ghoulish crowd, aren't you? Well, you're going to be disappointed, because I know very little about the hand. It came from Milan, by post, in a package tied with a red ribbon, yes. No one knows who sent it to Dori or why she hid it away at the bottom of a freezer rather than taking it to the police. It's a secret that she took with her to the grave, along with so many others. Yes, those are the facts: Gaetano Iabichino's handless corpse was found in his bathtub and the remains of the hand were found much later in Dori's basement: the bones that weren't burned in the fire the kids set. Those are the only sure things. Maybe Dori had her ex-husband killed. Maybe not. Not even Interpol could find that out. What do you want me to say? I don't have an opinion. And if I did, I wouldn't want to tell it to you. The only thing I know is that lives, like clothes, are not always cut along a straight line. There's the door. It must be Estela. If I were you I wouldn't light that cigarette.

DEBTS

Thanks to Ramón Muñoz and to Wikipedia, who helped resolve some of my queries on matters of fact.

Lightning Source UK Ltd.
Milton Keynes UK
UKOW04f0424191017

311224UK00001B/168/P